For over an hour, Slocum had seen the hatless riders appear on the eastern horizon. They kept a parallel course with them. He could barely see the color of their mounts, but figured they were mostly paints and piebalds. They definitely had company out there.

"Indians, ain't they?" Sug asked quietly over the calls of noisy ravens.

"Yes, a handful," he said, wondering how much farther Ft. Supply was from their location. One thing worried him the most. If they ran, could they reach its sanctuary before their horses gave out?

"What will they try to do?" she asked.

"Cut us off I figure, if they can."

"What do you plan to do?" she asked.

"Keep moving," he said. "I want to choose the place we fight them, if we have to fight. Let's lope these horses awhile."

"Slocum, I don't want them to take me alive." She looked at him with pleading eyes from under the sombrero.

"I hear you," he said . . .

DON'T MISS THESE
ALL-ACTION WESTERN SERIES
FROM THE BERKLEY PUBLISHING GROUP

THE GUNSMITH by J. R. Roberts
Clint Adams was a legend among lawmen, outlaws, and ladies. They called him . . . the Gunsmith.

LONGARM by Tabor Evans
The popular long-running series about U.S. Deputy Marshal Long—his life, his loves, his fight for justice.

SLOCUM by Jake Logan
Today's longest-running action Western. John Slocum rides a deadly trail of hot blood and cold steel.

BUSHWHACKERS by B. J. Lanagan
An action-packed series by the creators of Longarm! The rousing adventures of the most brutal gang of cutthroats ever assembled—Quantrill's Raiders.

DIAMONDBACK by Guy Brewer
Dex Yancey is Diamondback, a southern gentleman turned con man when his brother cheats him out of the family fortune. Ladies love him. Gamblers hate him. But nobody pulls one over on Dex . . .

WILDGUN by Jack Hanson
Will Barlow's continuing search for his daughter, kidnapped by the Blackfeet Indians who slaughtered the rest of his family.

SLOCUM
AND THE BLUE-EYED HOSTAGE

JOVE BOOKS, NEW YORK

This is a work of fiction. Names, characters, places, and incidents are either the product of the author's imagination or are used fictitiously, and any resemblance to actual persons, living or dead, business establishments, events, or locales is entirely coincidental.

SLOCUM AND THE BLUE-EYED HOSTAGE

A Jove Book / published by arrangement with
the author

PRINTING HISTORY
Jove edition / April 2001

All rights reserved.
Copyright © 2001 by Penguin Putnam Inc.
This book, or parts thereof, may not be reproduced in
any form without permission.
For information address: The Berkley Publishing Group,
a division of Penguin Putnam Inc.,
375 Hudson Street, New York, New York 10014.

The Penguin Putnam Inc. World Wide Web site address is
http://www.penguinputnam.com

ISBN: 0-515-13045-1

A JOVE BOOK®
Jove Books are published by The Berkley Publishing Group,
a division of Penguin Putnam Inc.,
375 Hudson Street, New York, New York 10014.
JOVE and the "J" design
are trademarks belonging to Penguin Putnam Inc.

PRINTED IN THE UNITED STATES OF AMERICA

10 9 8 7 6 5 4 3 2 1

1

He couldn't clear his head enough to wake up. Someone was talking to him, but she sounded far away, or was whispering so quietly her words seemed slurred. He jerked himself to a sitting position from under the blankets, and her firm hand caught his bare shoulder.

"Don Reyas is outside and wants to talk to you," she hissed in his ear.

He frowned at her, then impatiently asked, *"Que quiere?"*

"The richest man in the Espanola Valley. A big trader." She rose to her feet and shook out his pants for him to put on.

"What's he want from me?" Damn, it must be past sunup. He threw back the blankets, and their warmth quickly evaporated as the chill in the room found his bare skin. He rose to his feet, and through his dry eyes, he could see out the small window. Shafts of golden sunlight filtered through the cottonwoods. He had slept too hard the night before. Exhaling through his nose, he rose and put on the fresh shirt that she handed him. Then, to collect his thoughts, he combed his hair back through his fingers and reflected for a second on what he must do about this visitor.

"What does he want?" he asked again.

"I don't know, but he came by himself," she said, sounding taken aback by the man's presence in her yard.

"What's that mean?"

"He usually has some of his men riding with him. He has a *segundo* and many men on his payroll."

Slocum ran his calloused palm over his neck and then his smooth-shaven cheek. With his sleep-dulled mind, he was not quite his keenest self. He drew a deep breath and quickly pulled on his pants. Then he swept up the gunbelt off the ladder-back chair and strapped it on his waist.

Hatless and barefoot, he went to the doorway after her. He ducked under the low lintel to go outside, and spotted the fine sorrel horse under the giant cottonwood in her yard. The animal looked to be one of a kind, with a muscular sleek form that indicated speed and endurance.

"Señor Reyas, this is the man you seek. Slocum, this is the Don." She looked at the two of them as if someone should dismiss her. At the man's nod, without another word, she picked up a handful of her colorful skirt and went back inside her adobe casa.

"Good morning," Reyas said. He had a warm smile, under a small mustache trimmed neat and very proper. Soft black kidskin boots, handmade, no doubt in Santa Fe by the best cobbler. He wore pleated whipcord pants. The gold braid on the matching brown jacket was the real stuff. His flat-crowned hat was made of the finest beaver felt. Don Reyas dressed the part of a very rich man. Something about him, perhaps his openness, signaled to Slocum that this man was real. Slocum trusted his first instinct about people.

"Good morning," Slocum said, his mouth pleading for a good snort of fiery mescal. "We've never met before. I wondered why you asked for me."

"Now is a good time for us to meet. Can we visit, Señor?"

"I reckon so. We can sit over there," Slocum said, indicating the seat beside the huge gnarled cottonwood trunk.

"Very good. I hope I did not disturb your sleep."

"Doesn't matter, I'm up now." He could use a drink, but he'd better see about this Reyas business first. The soles of his bare feet were tender from the sticks and sharp stones strewn on the ground.

"You know that I am a trader?" They sat side by side on the slatted bench.

Slocum nodded.

"I am what you gringos call a Comanchero. I trade with the Comanches and have been in their camps many times. My grandfather and father have gone there before me. Does that bother you?"

Slocum shook his head. Whatever Reyas did for a living was his business, and as long as he wasn't raping, robbing, or murdering other humans, Slocum couldn't care less.

"It is a dangerous business, Señor. Sometimes, when you mess with the tiger, he bites you."

Slocum rubbed his index finger over his upper lip to quell an itch. He waited for the man to continue. Reyas spoke so clearly, so precisely, that Slocum knew all this explanation had a purpose. What was it?

"The army has banned us from trading with them," said Reyas. "They have pulled all our licenses. For centuries, my family has traded with the Iteha under the King of Spain, under the Mexican government, and even under the federal one. Now the army says no more permits. None of the old licenses are any good either. No one must trade with these wild people until they go to the reservation."

"I can't fix that. I know no one in office around here," Slocum said. If this man thought he had any power to change government or army policy, he was badly mistaken.

"Señor . . ."

"Slocum."

"Slocum, I am not afraid of sneaking past the army at Ft. Union. I am not afraid of the toughest Comanche out there, but my lovely wife Rosa has talked to a witch, who says if I do not hire a gringo *pistolero* to guard me, that my life will be taken on this trip."

Delores cleared her throat from a distance to get their attention. Slocum blinked at her in the fluttering light that danced through the cottonwood leaves. She carried a tray with coffee and food.

Slocum waved her over, and she set it between them.

"There is coffee and sugar, Don Reyas."

"*Gracias,* Delores," he said, and smiled at her.

"I will leave you. There is some honey and sopaipillas too."

"You are a wonderful hostess." Reyas saluted her.

"Thanks," Slocum managed with a warm, thick mug cradled in his hands. He watched through the coffee vapors as she moved back to her doorway barefoot. Such a wonderful shapely body underneath that colorful dress. He had thoroughly enjoyed his stopover in the village of Trucas.

"You have not said if you would work as a *pistolero* for me," Reyas reminded him.

"You have not mentioned money."

"We will be gone perhaps two months. How does two-fifty sound?"

"Sounds like too much money, but I would have asked that much."

"How soon can you leave?" Reyas asked, never flinching about the sum.

Damn, he didn't ask enough from the man. "I need to shoe my horse."

"No, I have a half brother to this sorrel that you may ride. A gray horse. Is that all right?"

"If he's half brother to *him* and out of a jenny, I would ride him." Slocum grinned at his words. Why, the horse would ride like an angel with wings if he was only half as good as that flaxen-maned sorrel looked to Slocum.

"Eagle is shod and waiting," Reyas said. "Rest your horse here. If Delores does not have feed enough for him while we are gone, one of my men will take him to my ranch until you return, and he will be too fat."

"Meaning you want to leave right now?" He waited for the man's reply.

"Yes. I know there is not much time for good-byes, but already my *Caritas* snake towards the caprock."

"They're already gone by Ft. Union?"

"Oh, they passed there at night and wiped out all their tracks. The army never knows when they go by."

"Don Reyas, I can be ready in thirty minutes." Slocum sipped some of the scalding coffee, and almost choked when Reyas made a loud shrill whistle. A dark-faced man on horseback charged into the yard, leading a dancing gray pony.

"Your horse, Señor—I mean, Slocum," Reyas said.

Regretting his bare feet, Slocum walked around the proud animal and examined him. His head was high, his ears were pinned forward, and his well-combed mane waved unfurled as he danced back and forth anxiously on his lead rope. His hide was sleek as a mole, and powerful muscles rippled beneath the surface. He was a royal horse, with the wind of desert barb breeding. He was light-footed on his striped gray and white hooves, which had been recently trimmed and shod.

"Will he do?" Reyas asked.

Slocum nodded in approval, then went back and downed his coffee. "I'll get my things and saddle."

"No rush," Reyas said, and began to talk to his man on horseback, who was holding the gray's lead rope.

"What does he want?" Delores asked when Slocum entered her small house.

Anxious to get into his boots, he brushed off his soles, put on socks, and soon pushed his toes deep in the vamps of his boots. He worked each foot until comfortable in the leather confines. Stomping his heels, he nodded in satisfaction and turned to answer her question.

"He needs me to ride with him. I'm going to be gone

for a while. Can you feed my buckskin? Otherwise his man will take him to his ranch."

"I will care for him."

"I know, I know. You're wondering why he came and asked me." Slocum searched about for his gear, still taken aback by the man's generous offer. "Says his wife was told by a witch that he must have a gringo guard on this trip or he will be killed."

"You are riding out there with the Comanches?" She crossed herself, closed her eyes, and began to softly pray to the Virgin Mary.

"I'll be fine. I've been in their camps before. I've traded some with them."

"I will burn a candle—no, two of them at the shrine, until you return."

"Good! I may need the protection. Here is all the money I have," he said, putting nearly thirty dollars in her hands.

"You will need some of this money?" She gave him a questioning look.

"No, I will let the Don take care of me."

She hurriedly spilled the money on the brown tabletop, and then she threw her arms around his neck. Tears filled her brown eyes.

"I told you that I'd have to leave any day," he reminded her. "This was a good visit. We have had time to talk."

She buried her face in his shirt and sobbed. "I will miss you, Slocum. Be careful, and I will pray for your safety."

"I may need that. But I'll be back. Just remember, anyone shows up asking about me, tell them I rode on."

"The one who rides the spotted horse?" She nodded her head as if she remembered the man.

"Yes, Lyle and his brother Ferd Abbott. Don't tell them any more than that, though they might end up Comanche stew if they follow us out on the Llano Estacado."

"Those men have been here before in this village asking about you."

"Good, you know them. They're bounty hunters. Send

them to San Francisco. No." He had a second thought.
"They might come back and hurt you."

"Why don't they quit tracking you?" She looked with
pain-filled wet eyes at him.

"A rich man in Ft. Scott, Kansas, pays their bills. He
blames me for his son's death. It happened long, long ago,"
he said as he swept up his Texas saddle and pads. With
them on his arm, he headed for the door. "Thanks for your
kindness and your good company," he said as he ducked
down for the doorway.

"You are a *mucho hombre* to darken my door. Come
back and soon."

"I'll try, Delores, I'll try."

He soon had his pads and saddle cinched on the gray,
and the animal settled down as if he knew his work was
about to begin. Delores brought out an extra tight-woven
cotton blanket for Slocum to tie inside his bedroll.

"Sometimes it gets cold out there, they say," she warned
him.

He nodded, bent over, and kissed her soft lips. Then they
parted. He swung in the saddle and nodded to Reyas.
"Ready to ride."

The smaller man tore out the gate of her yard on his
dashing sorrel. Slocum waved to her, jerked down his hat
brim, and sent the gray after him. The experience of the
powerful horse between his knees made his heart race as
he tore down the cottonwood-shaded road to catch Don
Reyas. This would be some challenge. The man he was to
protect might have too fast a horse for him to keep up with.
But then Slocum gave the gray his head, and the rush of
speed came like a cannonball. Soon, he began to close in
on the sorrel. Effortlessly, the animal reached further with
each stride to make greater and greater gains on the sorrel.

Slocum finally drew up his gray beside Reyas, who had
reined back his animal. They both settled into a long lope.

"You are hard on road chickens," Slocum said, teasing
him about the fighting fowl picking in the dust that were

forced to fly out of his path in a great flutter of feathers.

"I cleared two screaming sows from the road for you too," Reyas said, then threw back his head and laughed. "Good horses, fine weather, we have the best of this world, my friend."

A juniper-scented wind in his face, Slocum nodded to agree. For two hundred fifty bucks, he could stand it for two months . . . being a Comanchero.

2

The high-pitched complaints of the squeaking caritas wheels carried above the stiff wind. Dour oxen under their yokes plodded along on the dim road cut through the curly brown buffalo grass. The powerful gray danced between Slocum's knees. The gelding's ancestry ran back to the barb's invasion of Spain. The Moors had brought these bloodlines to the Iberian Peninsula centuries before. Slocum could recall reading about them as a boy growing up in Georgia.

He'd once watched them being unloaded off a sailing ship. A loudmouthed man had extolled their origin and how they would be auctioned at the next racing meet. Slocum's father had rather curtly told him and his brother that the horses were stolen. The desert people never sold their horses. They sold their daughters, but never their great animals.

Slocum could recall his youthful mind wandering as he looked at the seagulls diving into the calm harbor waters to feed. How did his father know such things? He had never been there—to Africa or wherever these people lived. Perhaps when Slocum grew older and wiser, he too could look at such proud horses and announce that they were stolen.

"John! John! We're ready to go!" his father shouted with impatience. Slocum flung a last clamshell out at the blue water, then ran hard to the buggy.

"Will they bring much money?" he asked as his father bruskly boosted him by the seat of his pants into the carriage.

"What?" his father asked, obviously distracted.

"Those fine horses back there."

"They will bring perhaps thousands, if there are enough fools at the auction with more money than they have good sense."

"I would sure like to have one of those horses," Slocum said, then rather than listen to a long lecture from his father on good sense, added, "When I have lots of money of my own."

"Hmm," his father snorted. "There will be more important things in your life, I hope, by then than buying dancing ponies."

The vision of those horses being unloaded on the dock lasted him through the war years. Several officers rode such fine animals. But by the end of the conflict, the dancing ponies, like the brave young men of the South, were all gone like smoke on the wind.

Don Reyas, riding beside him, broke into his thoughts when he spoke. "We should soon reach the camp of Black Horn, unless he is away chasing buffalo or raiding in Texas."

Slocum agreed. He took off his felt hat and wiped his gritty, wet forehead on his sleeve, thinking about the village they would find ahead. Comanches lived in small bands, moving with their herds of horses to fresh grass and to find the buffalo. Each camp had a chief, usually chosen for his prowess in war and hunting. While they used lodge-pole tepees made of twenty buffalo skins, they lacked the refined culture of other Plains tribes like the Cheyenne or even the Sioux.

Iteha or "the People," as they called themselves, were a

man's society. Women were subservient, and must not look attractive to another man, or their husbands would cut their noses off for adultery. Slocum could recall the filthy women laboring with hides and chores. Their hair was cut close, and they were dressed in rags for clothing. None of them ever looked up at him, their gazes lowered to the ground. Even before puberty, little girls were forced into polygamous marriages with older men.

He rubbed his calloused hand over the beard stubble on his chin. There wouldn't be much woman-watching ahead for him. Just as well. He had to keep his eye on Reyas.

"Look for captives," Reyas said. "Sometimes there are slaves that can be ransomed for good sums."

"I will," Slocum agreed.

"The best thing we can trade for is mules. I can sell many mules."

"The Comanche breed them?" Slocum asked, checking over the plodding oxen and the long train. Seeing nothing out of place, he turned back.

"Yes, they breed some and they steal some. Over the years, my mule trading has been more profitable than the buffalo hides, but now the hides are bringing much more money than they used to."

"You sell the mules to the army?" Slocum asked, mildly amused by the fact the U.S. Army might be using Comanche mules to chase them with.

"I sell them to traders who take them back up the Santa Fe Trail and sell them as good Missouri mules."

"Really?"

"Yes. Once I saw a particular mule in harness in Santa Fe. He had an unusual white scar on his butt that I recognized. It was a mule I'd traded for the year before from the Comanche. When I spoke to the teamster and asked him about the animal, he said, 'That mule's never been West before. Born and raised in Missouri, mister, on a farm back there.' "

"You got him from the Comanche?"

"Yes."

With a shake of his head, Slocum excused himself and rode to the rise. Ahead, he could see, in a veil of smoke, the lodge poles sticking out of the tepee covers. The gray-sided tepees, even at this distance, bore none of the colorful painting other Plains Indians decorated theirs with.

Over the eternal wind, he could hear the dogs barking, and could see the men hurriedly mounting up. Their war cries carried faintly. Soon they would be charging out to meet the friend or foe that approached them.

He turned the gray and short-loped him back to Don Reyas. Juarez, the wagon boss, was with him on a glossy bay that shone like polished oak. The gelding carried himself Morgan style, and Slocum suspected the animal bore such blood. A powerfully built man wearing a red head rag instead of a sombrero, Juarez nodded solemnly when Slocum told them about the bucks headed for them.

"Good. My man Juarez does not trust Black Horn," Reyas said. "He considers him too moody and says we must be careful not to offend him."

Slocum agreed to be careful as he reined up the prancing gray to settle him. Obviously the animal was upset by the the war cries headed toward them. Horses could hear much better than a man.

"You're the boss. Whatever you say," Slocum said to Reyas. For his part, all Comanches were like sidewinders, quick to strike without warning and deadly.

"Thanks, Juarez," Reyas said, and dismissed him. The man galloped off on the Morgan to the rear of the train.

Reyas turned back to Slocum. "He has everyone alerted that we must be on our guard at this camp."

Eagle flinched underneath him at the first pop of a rifle. Slocum set him down, and gave his hat brim a tug to save it from the gust of wind that threatened it. The hard-riding bucks, naked save for loincloths, charged past them in a stream on both sides of the train, yipping like coyotes and firing their arms in the sky. No one rode like a Comanche.

They impressed Slocum all over again. Without a saddle, they could be anywhere on the back of a running horse, over the side, in a jockey's position, or dangerously far back, but they were never unseated, and rode fearlessly. He had seen a fallen Comanche in a wagon train attack jump up, grab a passing horse's tail, and vault up behind another rider.

Under the hot midday sun, he watched the howling bucks with edgy concern as they came back on their hard-breathing ponies and the chief rode up to Reyas. He wore a black horn in the center of the buffalo-hide cap tied under his chin with straps. His deep-lined face had a black hue, and his dark eyes resembled chunks of pure coal. The hard set to his thin mouth made him look no more friendly.

"You come to trade?" he asked, holding a new-looking repeater balanced on his knee. The black-and-white piebald he rode was a broad-chested, full stallion who tried to pick a fight with Reyas's sorrel. The animal's impatient scream and foot-stomping carried across the grassland.

Black Horn looked undisturbed by the horse's action, and Don Reyas mildly nodded in reply. "We have many trade goods. It is hard to avoid the blue coats these days. We come at much risk to trade with our allies, the Iteha."

"I know. Who is this one rides with you?" Black Horn demanded, pulling down his stallion with a sliver-mounted spade bit. Sunlight reflected off the hammered coin neck-lace around the chief's neck.

"He is my helper."

"What is your name, helper?"

"Slocum."

"Slo-cum." Black Horn pronounced it slowly in two syllables. "Have we met before?"

Slocum shook his head.

"Then why are you so familiar to me? Have we fought?"

"No. But they say all white men look alike." Slocum shrugged off his concern.

Black Horn laughed aloud and then nodded. "Maybe so."

The laughter of this broad-chested man of medium height did not sound real. He would do to keep a good eye on.

"Do you have goods for the women?" Black Horn asked Reyas.

"Yes, beads, cloth, candy, spoons, pots, and knives."

"Did you bring plenty of bread?"

"Yes."

"Good. We will talk about things that you want to trade for."

"Skins without holes in them." Reyas looked over at the man.

Slocum felt better. The rest of the bucks had fallen into riding beside the wagons. They acted less warlike as Reyas continued his list of goods he would trade for. "I would trade for mules."

"You would take money?"

Slocum heard the word *money,* and noticed a small flicker in the trader's look. Then Reyas spoke quickly as if nothing was out of place. "Yes, I will take money. You have much of it?"

Black Horn nodded smugly, but he never mentioned the amount or the source of his wealth. Obviously the headman had a pile of it. Indians were not stupid, and they quickly learned about the power of coins and bills.

When they reached the edge of the camp, a boy from the wagon train took Eagle and the sorrel from them, while a Comanche woman in tattered rags rushed up and led off Black Horn's squealing piebald. Carefully, she held the reins close to the bit, and walked beside his head to avoid a striking forehoof.

"Come with me," Black Horn said, and led them through the camp. Slocum and Reyas followed the man, who acted like a king striding through his court in the midday sun. Obviously, he wanted everyone to see how he led these white eyes to his tepee.

On their hands and knees, two women in filthy dresses worked fleshing a large green buffalo hide on the ground.

Black Horn went over to them, grasped one of them unexpectedly by the short hair on her head, and jerked her face up. Then a cruel smile crossed his thin lips as he used his other hand to jerk out his rust-colored, half-erect dick from his loincloth.

"Take it!" he ordered, and shoved it between her lips. The woman's eyes closed in pain. But obediently, she dropped the small knife and began to fondle his scrotum with her fingers. Her cheeks drew in with her efforts. Black Horn humped his butt hard toward her face.

Slocum and Don Reyas were forced to stand and watch him show off. Black Horn's hard face soon showed signs of pleasure, and he gave a loud grunt and came. Then quickly he reached down and grasped her nose tightly between his fingers, forcing her to swallow his cum.

She began choking and gagging. He gave her a swift kick in the side with his moccasin and spilled her onto the green hide. Her eyes glared back like diamonds at her tormentor.

"Good enough for you," Black Horn said with disdain, and put his privates back in the breechcloth. With his chest puffed out, he nodded to the two men to continue with him toward his large tepee.

When Slocum started past the woman, he heard her suck in her breath and growl, "You gawdamn son of a bitch! Someday I'll cut that off and stuff it down your throat!"

Despite the hot sun, her threat sent a cold chill up his spine. A white captive, no doubt. Then he realized as he walked beside Reyas, not daring to look back at her, that those glaring eyes she'd flashed at Black Horn were blue.

3

A squaw squatted to pee on the ground as they approached the chief's tepee. Then she quickly rose and went back inside the opening. The familiar strong visceral-fecal smell of their camp settled in Slocum's nose. A typical stinking Comanche village. Bones and black, sun-dried gut remains were strewn about on the ground. One had to be careful where one stepped. A handful of mangy curs with cowardly growls in their throats slinked around to stay out of reach of a fast kick or quirt.

"Good that you came," Black Horn announced, and then ducked to go into his lodge. "We must soon move and find the horses new grass."

Reyas removed his hat to go inside, and Slocum gave a last look around. All the shabby-dressed women in camp were in a tither, gossiping about the train's arrival. Bashful children wearing only shabby shirts, their genders exposed, peeked at him from behind women's skirts.

Juarez was already busy setting up their camp at a good distance from the Comanches for reasons of safety. Slocum took a good breath of the fresh wind, and went inside filled with dread.

Reyas indicated Slocum should take a seat beside him

on the worn buffalo hides strewn on the ground for a carpet. Soft light from the outside could be seen through the semi-translucent skins. A small fire in the center circle gave off the sharp smell of buffalo chips. Two women were busy moving iron kettles around on the coals.

Black Horn passed a pipe around for them to smoke. Reyas presented the chief with a necklace of turquoise stones and silver beads strung on a leather cord. Black Horn put it around his neck with a nod of approval.

"You have guns like this?" he asked, patting the new-model Winchester across his lap.

Reyas shook his head. "No. The gringos won't sell them to me."

"Can you steal them?"

Reyas shook his head. "They watch them too close."

Slocum sat crossed-legged. The whang of the pipe's smoke and the spittle in the stem still tasted bitter on his tongue. Obviously Reyas did not wish to supply the Comanche with repeating rifles. It was bad enough that the man broke the law, coming out there at great risk and trading goods without a license, but to trade the Comanches new firearms would be a much more serious crime, meriting more than a small fine. If the military even suspected that the traders had armed the Iteha with repeaters, it would be a much greater offense, and their prison time would be long.

"Will some white man trade such guns for money?" Black Horn said, sounding upset that Reyas had rebuffed him.

The Don shook his head. "I have many goods that the Comanche need, but the rifles, I cannot bring them to you."

"Then tell me where I must go to find them."

Reyas shot a questioning look at Slocum, and they both shook their heads. He turned back. "There may be some traders who would sell them, but they would be fools. We don't know of such men."

"I have four Texas captives," Black Horn said, as if they were his ace in the hole for weapons.

"Who are they?" Reyas asked.

"I will show them to you. Are they worth rifles?"

Reyas made a glum face. "I would have to see them and who they are. Some white people have no money, no guns to pay for their children's return."

Slocum had the notion that Black Horn wanted new rifles at any price. The hard-faced chief seated facing them would get his way too, either with Reyas or someone else.

Black Horn said something guttural in Comanche to the two waiting women squatted at the side. They rose and went to the packs. Soon, with much effort, they lugged over a Wells Fargo express box to set before them. The lock, busted open, hung down like a dog's lolling tongue.

Impatiently, Black Horn waved the women away and rose to his knees. A sly smile spread over the deep lines in his face. He lifted the lid and exposed the gold coins that glowed in the low light.

Reyas drew a deep breath, settled back, and nodded in approval. Black Horn looked with smug contempt at Slocum, who issued a low "Yes."

"How many guns will you bring me," Black Horn shouted, "for this box?"

Slocum closed his eyes to savor the moment. *My gawd, my gawd, there must be a fortune in that strongbox.* No telling how or where it came from. It was blood money, no doubt, but how did Black Horn ever get his hands on it? They were dealing with a dangerous man, with big plans to increase his effectiveness in warfare with more fire-power.

"I will speak to the captives," Reyas said. "Send them to my camp."

"This will not buy guns?" Black Horn asked, letting a handful of the double eagles stream down onto the others.

"Some—yes, someone will sell you guns for a big enough price." Reyas shook his head. "I fear the army and what they would do to my people if they learned of it. But there are white men who will bring you those guns when they learn how rich Black Horn is."

"Send them to see me!" he said through his bared yellow teeth.

With the matter settled for the moment, Reyas excused himself and Slocum. They ducked outside, and Slocum was grateful for fresher air when he straightened up outside the tepee's door.

"Where in the hell did that money come from?" Reyas asked, glancing back to be certain they were alone.

"I heard of an express robbery in Colorado a few years ago, and the robbers, who made a big take, rode south. No one ever heard of them or the loot again."

"Think the Comanches got them?"

"Didn't matter who did. Folks figured the outlaws fell into Indian hands. More than likely the Cheyenne or a Kiowa war party got them that far north. They didn't want the gold and so they left the box. Black Horn learns about it, rides up, gets the box, and he's ready to buy new repeaters."

"Make lots of sense," Reyas agreed.

"Must be two fortunes in that damn strongbox." Slocum drew a deep breath, grateful to be out of the foul-smelling tepee. He spat. Smoking that peace pipe had his tongue raw.

"But there's not enough there for me to violate the ban against guns," said Reyas.

Slocum agreed . . . but someone would sell them. As Reyas had said, the word would soon be out that Black Horn had plenty of cash for repeaters.

"Take me away from this stinking place!" It was Blue Eyes, blocking their path with a small skinning knife clutched in her fist.

"Where is your home?" Reyas asked.

"Hell with my home. It's down in Texas. They wouldn't have me back. Look at me, I am soiled. They wouldn't have me under their roof again. Take me out of here. Somehow I will pay you back."

"I will see what I can do," Reyas said.

She looked past them to be certain no one was observing them, then continued. "You're white men. Save me from these rutting savages. You see how they treat white women." Quickly she dropped to her knees and went back to fleshing the green hide.

The two men exchanged hard looks. Slocum wondered how they would ever get her away. Perhaps she would be among the ones Black Horn offered Reyas, but in the back of his mind, he doubted it. There was some kind of war going on between Blue Eyes and Black Horn. If Slocum wanted his scalp, he'd better avoid becoming involved in it. His job was to protect Don Reyas, not save white slaves.

He looked the camp over. There was nothing hostile or threatening, but that could change any second with these savages. They didn't need a good reason to become pissed off. He and Reyas returned to their camp.

Already some of the women were there, trading a buffalo robe for three large round loaves of bread. Squaws, with their laughing, excited children gathered around them, were seated on the ground cross-legged and tearing into the loaves. Slocum watched them pass out shreds of bread to small hands.

"You look in deep thought," Slocum said to Reyas, feeling relieved they were back among their own at last.

Reyas shook his head. "That was a large sum of money in that box."

"Those rifles he wants, they'd kill a lot of innocent people too."

"Yes, some of mine too, no doubt. Let's find a drink. I need something to clear my head and mouth."

Slocum agreed, and looked back at the tepees. He couldn't get over the plea of Blue Eyes.

4

In the midday sun, Vinegar Malloy, known as Vin, sat at the base of a stinking mountainous pile of buffalo hides in Ft. Dodge, busy dickering for some pussy with a small dirty-faced squaw.

"Have another drink." He held out the quart-sized crock toward her.

Her brown eyes flickered alive. Like a cat, she took the jug in both hands and threw her head back. Vin could swear she must have gulped down half of it. Hell, all he'd meant for her to have was a little swig. Damn, this was getting serious. He'd messed with her for a half hour, trying to get her to lie down and screw him. Wouldn't take him long to get through with her either. Why, the cramping in his left testicle was worse than a damn toothache. Must have been months since he'd had any.

He took back the jug, set it down beside him, and scooted closer to her. With their knees touching, he could smell her. Never mind the stink. He made some sign language at her, sliding a finger through the ring he made with the other hand.

She smiled at him like a damn dumb jackass. Did that mean yes or no? How the hell could he tell?

"You want to do it?" he asked, raising his voice.

She blinked her eyes, and he knew she didn't understand a damn word he had said. Beside himself with his need for some relief, he put his hand on her leg. She smiled. He drew a deep breath. Seducing her was going to take more time, since she didn't understand a word of English. He had no idea how Indians got other Indians to screw. Backus said they never kissed, and didn't believe in kissing. Vin never liked kissing anyway, but he'd kiss her dirty face if it would make her cooperate with him.

He soon had his hand exploring under her dirt-glazed buckskin skirt, and squeezed her bony knee. Made him feel better to have his fingers there. It wasn't far to her crotch. She gave him a small smile, and he gave her one back. He touched the skin on the inside of her upper leg, and she giggled out loud, which caused him to jerk it away.

She caught his hand and put it back there, to his surprise. He nodded in approval. He was finally getting somewhere with her. The damn whiskey must be working on her. She'd drunk enough of it. He let his fingers creep up until at last he felt her coarse pubic hair. She looked down and, to his amazement, raised up her butt for him. He used the opportunity to stick his middle finger inside her. Wow, things were moving right along. Breathing fast and fired up, he went to probing her as hard as he could. Her face unmoved by his actions, she reached over, grabbed the whiskey, and took another big gulp. When she let the jug down, some of the liquor ran out of the corner of her mouth and dripped off her chin.

"You want to fucky me?" she asked, plain as day.

"Hell, yes!" Vin swore. He jerked his finger out and went to tearing his gunbelt loose and his pants open. His heart raged and his breath grew short at the prospect of at long last sticking his old rod into her.

She lay back on the smelly hides and raised up her stiff leather skirt for him. At the sight of his dick, she lifted her head up and frowned at him. "You got plenty big one."

"Aw, shut up," he said, and scooted over on his knees to stick it inside her. He couldn't believe that the damn bitch spoke good English.

He lowered himself on her, stabbed it in place, and was soon humping the small woman. Man, it felt so good. By damn, he knew he would get in her sooner or later. Oh, he really needed for this to happen. He was so masterfully screwing his Indian love, she even closed her eyes in pleasure. The next thing he knew, someone had their arm around his shoulder and this guy's whiskey breath was right in Vin's face.

"Get off her! It's my turn now."

"Who in the gawdamned hell are you?" Vin shouted in disbelief. His empty stomach had a great rock forming in the center of it.

The bearded man took hold of Vin's shoulders and tried to wrestle him off her. Vin drew back and slugged him with all his might. The blow knocked the sumbitch away. Still in shock and disbelief at the intruder's boldness, Vin looked down at the squaw, whose brown eyes were big as silver dollars.

"Stay there. I ain't through screwing you," Vin said to her. Looking frightened and holding her dirty skirt up, she crawfished a little ways up the pile.

"Stay there," Vin said to her again as he twisted around, pinned down by his own pants wrapped around his knees. He reached out for his gunbelt with his gaze still on the stunned drunk. Hand over hand, Vin drew the holster up, and at last jerked out the Colt, an instant before the enraged man recovered and lunged for him. Vin jammed the pistol's muzzle in the man's gut and fired. It made a muffled sound, but the force of the bullet passing through the man lifted him off Vin and threw him on his back. Trying with his left hand to pull his pants up enough to allow him the freedom to move, Vin held the Colt ready to shoot the crazy sumbitch again.

In disbelief, he watched the wounded hulking form rise

to his feet with a roar in his throat. He lifted his arms up
to attack, and Vin blew him down with a second bullet.
Damn, the report of that last shot would sure draw a crowd.
He jerked up his pants, and managed to hang one of his
galluses over his shoulder. Then, in a panic-filled moment,
he swept up his felt hat and jammed it on his head. Whiskey
crock in one hand, the Colt and his holster in the other, he
took after the squaw, who only seconds before had disappeared around the end of the hide pile.

Running low, he scurried behind several parked wagons
and rigs. Then he heard a hiss, couldn't see anything, and
finally noticed her waving her hand for him to join her in
a small shed. He quickly looked around. No one in sight.
He took three long strides on his boot toes and was inside
the abandoned buyer's shed.

She quickly closed the door after him.

"Who in the hell was he?" he asked her.

She shook her head that she didn't know, then whipped
out a blanket onto the dirt floor and undid her skirt. She let
the garment fall to her feet, looking at him all the while.
Standing barefoot in only a stained deerskin shirt, with half
the fringe gone and a few beads sewn on the front that
barely reached her waist, she acted ready to submit to him.
He shook his head in disbelief. She wanted more. Before
the two of them did anything else, he wanted to check on
the goings-on outside. He turned and peeked out the crack
in the door. Men were running by and shouting about someone being shot.

He put the door latch in place. Satisfied they weren't
looking for him, he turned and grinned at her. Thinking
about sticking it in her twat again, he toed off his Coffee-
ville boots and then removed his pants. This time he aimed
to really enjoy her without interruptions. She dropped onto
her knees and with both hands lifted the crock to her mouth,
then took another big swig of his whiskey.

He removed his shirt, then paused to listen to more of
the noisy confusion going on outside.

"I seen the sumbitch ride off on a yellow horse!" someone shouted, and those words caused him to smile. More misinformation like that and he'd be home free. Hell, they must be gathering a posse out there.

"Which way did he go?" someone asked

"Thataway!"

"Gawdamnit! Get Buck and Tommy, Joe, we need to ride him down!"

Vin dropped on his knees and grinned at her. Then he took the whiskey jug from her and took a big snort of the fiery stuff for himself. It was almost all gone. The powerful liquor about took his breath away. She pulled him down, and her small fingers played with his half erection. Soon she had him hard, and raised her knees so he could insert it in her. He lifted the blouse to look at her small tits. Busy at last pounding it to her, he closed his eyes to the pleasure.

The hard rap on the shed door made him furious.

"Hey, who's in there?" someone asked, trying to see through the crack.

"Gawdamnit, get the hell out!" he shouted.

"You see who shot this fella over behind the pile?"

"Hell, no, and I don't give a gawdamn!"

"What're you doing in there anyway?"

"Trying to screw a damn Injun squaw. What do you think I'm doing? Now get the hell out of here!"

"Oh, I'm sorry," the intruder said in a small voice. Then, as he walked away, he shouted to someone else, "That fella in there, he don't know nothing about it."

In disgust, his erection gone, Vin gave up and lay down on his back beside her. It was no use. Both times he'd been interrupted. His peeker had gone limp. His left nut still hurt, and he was too damn discouraged to even try her again. Hell's fire, things always had a sorry way of working out for him.

"You got guns?" she asked, rolling over on her side and resting her hand on his belly in a friendly way.

"Got my Colt and a Sharps rifle on my horse to shoot buff with."

She shook her head, bracing it up with her elbow. "You got many new guns. 'Peaters?"

"Repeaters," he corrected her.

She nodded that that was what she meant, still looking at him.

"No. What do you want to do with them?"

"Chief Black Horn pay." She held up ten fingers.

"Ten what?" he asked.

She smiled and showed him the twenty-dollar gold piece strung on a rawhide string from around her neck.

"He will pay ten gold coins for every new repeater I get him?" Vin sucked in his breath at the notion.

"Has plenty money," she explained.

"Where did he get that kind of money?"

She held up three fingers. He nodded, then she held them sideways. He nodded again, still not sure what she meant. She made the sign of one, then another one, and a snake.

"What the hell is that?" He frowned impatiently at her.

"On box Black Horn got."

"Wells, Wells Fargo!" he said, unable to believe it. "Sweet Jesus, girl. He has a Wells Fargo box full of them twenty-dollar gold pieces?"

She nodded. He tackled her around the waist and hugged her. She smelled like she'd never, ever wiped her ass, but it made no difference. His chance to get rich had finally arrived. He began kissing her in his enthusiasm, and she went to jerking on his dick.

In minutes, he was hard as an iron shaft and was boring in her mine. Then at last, when he damn sure felt her side-walls contracting on him, his whole stem felt on fire. He came in a great, butt-sucking blast that left him too weak to get off her and lie down.

It was dark outside when he awoke. She was still there. His fingers touched her small butt. The need to relieve his swollen bladder was so great, he clumsily rose up, threw open the door, and began to piss in a great stream out into the starlit night.

He finally had the formula to all the riches in the world. It was in some pint-sized piece of Indian ass lying on that old blanket behind him. Hot damn. He at last had the key to all the money he would ever need. His stream still poured out in a great arc, giving him more relief than screwing her had. Find some rifles, then let her lead him to this Black Horn's camp, and he'd never need to work again. No more shooting another stinking buffalo or having to smell those stinking guts when he skinned them. He'd be rich enough to screw princesses, if he wanted to. Did princesses do that? He shook his tool and closed the door. Hell, they must. Indian princesses did it.

He awoke again at daybreak. If he bought all the guns at one time, say in Ft. Dodge, someone would get suspicious and report him to the authorities. There were enough notices around warning about selling firearms or whiskey to the hostiles. This Black Horn had to be a hostile. No, he needed a good source of those guns and some credit until he got back from selling them. Maybe he could buy several and only have to put a few on the credit. It was going to be delicate getting the weapons gathered, he decided. Maybe he could steal them, if he didn't get caught at it.

"Lets go get some grub," he said to her.

Looking half asleep, she pulled on her stained leather skirt and fastened it closed with lacing. Then she used her hand to push the shaggy ragged-cut hair back from her small face.

"You my squaw," he said, and pointed at her. "You *comprende?*"

She smiled big. He knew she understood what he meant.

He bought some food from an old woman in a wagon. Cold hard soda biscuits and a large mess of fire-cooked buffalo that wasn't bad. They ate it under a cottonwood close to the Arkansas. She went and filled his empty whiskey crock with river water for them to wash it down with.

"I've got a wagon," he said to her. "And I have a mule. Used it to haul in my hides. We'll need it to take them rifles down there to sell to Black Horn." She probably didn't understand a word of all he told her, but no matter, she was his ticket to becoming filthy rich.

"See," he said, "I've got this plan to get some more rifles. When it's dark, I'll tie old Clunny, my horse, up at the hitch rail beside some fella has a Winchester in his scabbard. I slip his rifle in my empty scabbard and get away with it." He gnawed on some more buffalo. "Ain't a bad idea, if we don't get caught. There's always that risk."

Night fell, and he made his way up Front Street, where the tent saloons and stores were lined up to do business with the buffalo hunters and soldiers from the fort. Each establishment was noisy with the hell-raisers. He could see the men's outlines on the yellow canvas walls illuminated by the lamps. Out in the street, he could hear the sounds of the hand organs and pianos from inside. He stopped to dismount, then acted like he was about to hitch his horse. Quick as a cat he filched a rifle, slipped it in his empty scabbard, and rode out like an ordinary buffalo hunter going about his business. With four rifles taken by midnight, he decided the town law would soon be on to him. He hid them for safekeeping under the floor of the scale house of Denver and Jennings, the biggest hide buyers in Kansas.

Back in the dark shack, he started figuring how to get more long guns and not draw suspicion. He could buy some next. He had the money from his hide sales and some credit with Whipple and Sons Hardware and General Merchandise. He lay beside the squaw. The strong aroma coming from his bed partner grew worse as he listened to the cicadas sizzling outside. He had some soap and a towel in his gear. She would fit in a girl's dress. Hell, they couldn't cost much. He'd go do that in the morning, get her a new dress and then a bath.

So, at first light, he walked into the mercantile, and picked out a dress that looked big enough and not too large.

He paid the frowning clerk and hurried out the door. He never stopped at the boy's words. "That dress sure won't fit *you!*"

Then he took the squaw, new dress, towel, and soap down to the Arkansas. Around the bend, he found a place for them to be alone. He began to undress. He took off his hat, then his gunbelt, pants, and shirt. He motioned for her to do the same, while he removed his one-piece long underwear. She obeyed him, and soon stood naked as a jaybird.

With a bar of soap in one hand and her hand in the other, he headed for the water. She held back, but he insisted, and dragged her along until she soon stood up to her knees in the dingy stream, looking very afraid. He still grasped her hand, and with his other hand sloshed some water on her. She danced away from him. He hung on to her, and in her effort to escape him, she slipped on the sandy bottom and fell down. Looking up in dismay, she sat on her butt, up to her small nipples in the water. Vin pulled her up, and used the opportunity to apply soap all over, and soon she was white with lather. He didn't spare an inch of her hide. Her efforts to make him stop were weak. He finally had her snowy white with lather from her knees to the top of her head.

Then he showed her how to rinse it away and left her to do it, while he went a little deeper in the river to wash himself. He looked up, and a twinge of fear grabbed him when two men rode up out of the willows. For an instant, he wondered about his handgun on the bank, but there was no time for that. He went on and lathered his chest as if all was well. They looked hard at the squaw first, but she ignored them, standing there half-frosted in soap, naked as Eve and using handfuls of water to remove it.

"Sorry to bother you, mister," one of the men said, "but someone stole four Winchesters last night. We're looking to see if the thief stashed them along the river." The man leaned over the saddle horn to talk to him while his partner tried to look away, obviously uncomfortable over the squaw's nakedness.

"We ain't seen none," Vin said, and soaped under his arms.

"No suspicious characters?"

"None."

"Damn, I wonder what they did with them," one said to the other.

"Damned if I know."

Vin tried to listen to their conversation as they rode off, but they were soon gone upriver.

"They don't know shit," he said to her under his breath, wading over and seeing that the soap was rinsed off. Her brown skin glowed. He pointed to the towel on the willow bush.

"Towel," she said.

"Yeah, it's a towel." In long strides through the water, he led her onto the bank. "Yes, dry with my towel." He used it on her, and then himself. He was half dried off before he suddenly realized she was putting back on her old clothes.

"No. Wait. New dress." He held up the new garment to her. Maybe if he had held a book up to her, she would have stared in the same shocked disbelief at it. "Dress's for you, girl."

He unbuttoned the front and held it up so she could slip her arms into it. Then he began to button the front for her. She pushed his hands away, and began to learn how to do it herself. After her fumbling, a few buttons were out of row, and he pointed to them as he redressed. She undid them, and soon had the line straight down the front. In a burst of gratitude she rushed over and hugged him. She smelled like soap. A lot better than the perfume she wore before he gave her the bath.

How in the hell would he get more rifles? Damn, four of them weren't enough to go trudging off down there with. He knew about a Spencer that a fella had that he could buy for a few bucks. Maybe he could buy some other rifles off the Ft. Dodge drunks needing money. But most of them were hunters and had single-shot Sharps, not repeaters. He needed killing power, not firepower.

He planned to see what he could buy without raising suspicion. Hell, if Black Horn didn't want Spencers—he could lump it. Who else would even take the risk to go down there with a wagon load of rifles? That red bastard better be glad that he was collecting them for him. Damn, it would be nice to be rich. He swung the towel on his shoulder and glanced over at his squaw. She needed something for her hair. Even washed, it still stuck out every which way like a porcupine. If she'd brush it a hundred strokes each day, it might lie down. He'd get her a hairbrush to do that. How in the hell would he ever teach her to count that high? Hell, he didn't know.

5

"How in the hell are you getting me out of here?"

Slocum half raised himself up on his elbows, blinked, then twitched his nose at the fecal smell. It was Blue Eyes. In the starlight, he could make her out. She was on her hands and knees underneath the wagon where Slocum lay in his bedroll. Whew, she sure needed a bath.

"How did you get here anyway?" He had no idea what time it was. Couldn't see the Big Dipper. Didn't matter. He was curious about her and how she had fallen into the hands of these Comanches.

"These damn Comanches made a raid down on the Brazos. I was at a dance that night with a boy. We were over at a neighbor's place. We never knew them red devils were about. We started for home, under a full moon, must have run into twenty of them on the road. He—Troy never stood a chance. I whipped the mare that I was on and got away. Outran them. Thought I'd beat them, but when I got home, they'd burned the place to the ground. I saw my mother facedown in the ashes. Kid brother Abe lying there in the moonlight, all scalped and bloody. My paw and older brother Hale weren't home—off moving some cattle that they bought."

She bellied down on the ground beside his bedroll, took a blade of grass, and chewed on it. "About that time that red bastard Black Horn rode in, swept me up, and here I am."

"What do they call you?" he asked, leaning back on his elbows to consider her.

"Blue Bonnet in Comanche."

"No, your given name?"

"Safra, Safra Maude Irons."

"You want to go back to Texas? To home?"

"Aw, come on. I've been raped by twenty Comanche or more. Be lucky if I don't have one of them red sons a bitches in my belly right now. I know them Irons men. They'll say, why did she let them rape her? Must be her fault."

Slocum rubbed his forehead with his fingertips, and small crinkles of dirt turned up under his touch. What could he do for her? Where would she fit in? He understood her frankness. There was no place in that kind of Texas society for a woman soiled by redskins, regardless of her real innocence.

"They call you Safra?"

"No, Sug was what they called me. Short for Sugar."

"Sug, if I can't get you out this time, I'll be back for you."

"You ain't just telling me that, are you?" She drew the straw from her mouth and waited for his word.

He shook his head. "I'm not lying to you. But first I have to see Don Reyas safely back home. I made him a promise to guard him this trip. After that I'll come back for you, if he can't get you freed."

"Mister . . ." She rose up on her hands and knees. "You won't regret it. I can promise your sweet ass, you won't regret it."

"I'll be coming for you, Sug."

She nodded that she'd heard him, then retreated out backward on her hands and knees, stuck the straw back in her mouth, and moved off in the starlight. Slocum eased himself out of his bedroll. Standing beside the wagon, he watched her dark form slip back into the village.

Satisfied she was safely in her place, he went to the edge of the Comanchero camp, where the saddle horses were hitched on a picket line. He knew one of their guard sat nearby in the dark with a rifle ready to defend them.

Slocum dropped to his heels and rolled one from the makings. He shielded the match, drew on his cigarette. The smoke tasted rewarding. Then he heard the footsteps of someone coming to join him.

"A visitor awaken you tonight?" Juarez asked, sounding amused. Armed with a repeater laid over his knees, he squatted beside Slocum.

"Yes, a white captive who wants out."

"Figured so. Years ago, a girl came to me one night like that when we were trading at a Comanche camp. She was from Chihuahua. Said her father was very rich. Said her name was Maria Vasquez Peralta and would I please ransom her." Juarez turned his ear to the gentle night wind as if testing the sounds. Then satisfied nothing was wrong, he continued.

"She had been taken to be the wife of a big Comanche called Tall Tree. My, she was such a beautiful girl. Tall Tree told me that I must bring him twenty horses for her. So I went back home to the Espanola Valley and borrowed all the money I could to buy horses. My friends, they even gave me some. I finally had them and rushed back to find the band. I rode night and day."

Slocum looked over and saw the man's eyes narrow. "When I finally found his camp, there was no sign of her."

"What had happened to her?"

"She'd bled to death when he cut off her nose for being adulterous with me."

Slocum nodded. "I know it is a perilous existence for any white woman among these people."

"Don't get your hopes too high, and may the Virgin

Mary protect her until you can save her," Juarez said, then quickly crossed himself and rose to his feet. His moccasins crossed the curly grass as he went to check on something else.

Slocum ground the last of the butt out. How would he attempt to get her freed? If he showed very much interest in her, Black Horn might kill or maim her. Comanches could be vengeful for the slightest reason. There was no need to endanger her until he could move. Being forced to hold back grated on him, but he needed restraint and lots of it if his plan to rescue her would ever work.

In the morning, two older squaws herded the four Tejas children captives to the trades' camp for inspection. The children were sunbaked brown and dirty, and almost looked like the offspring of the two Indian women. A boy of perhaps seven or eight stood before Don Reyas. In a leather shirt that barely reached past his navel, his small privates exposed, he stood sucking his thumb and looking uncomfortable. The scars on his legs could be seen through the dirt.

"What is your name?" Reyas softly asked him with Slocum standing alongside.

"Wayne," the boy answered.

"Where does your family live?"

Wayne cocked one eye at him and closed the other. "On a ranch."

"Near what town?"

The boy shrugged his shoulders as if he didn't know.

"What is your father's name?" Slocum asked.

"Paw."

"They call you Wayne Smith or Wayne Jones?" Slocum asked, wondering how to reach into this child's darkened mind for his identity.

"Them Comanches call me—" The guttural word he gave them was lost on the two men.

"No, we need you father's name," Reyas said.

The boy reached down and scratched his scrotum as if

he could not hold off any longer and something was biting him down there. Then he shook his head. "Ain't no need to know his name, mister. I can't remember." Then his eyes narrowed. "Besides, they're all dead now—they killed all of them."

"All of them?" Reyas asked softly.

"Killed my brother Gabriel too, 'cause he cried. I don't ever cry."

"If I could buy you, would you go with us to my ranch, Wayne?"

"Could I wear pants?"

Reyas nodded. "Yes, you could."

"I'd go with you then."

The next was a small girl, and she hugged an older one of perhaps nine. Obviously, learning the little one's origin would be hard. Reyas spoke to the older girl who held her.

"What is your name?"

"Mary Martin Mc—Mc something, mister. I used to know it. I lived on Cedar Creek and we used the Two L branding iron. I can make it in the dust if you want me to. This young'un here is Sarie, she don't know nothing but to hide, so she don't get whipped. You know whipping used to hurt me too?"

"It doesn't hurt now, Mary?" Reyas asked.

She shook her head. "But we'd sure go with you to your ranch. I can do lots of work too."

Reyas reached out and ruffled her hair. "I will try to buy you two."

"Who are you?" the trader asked the last youth, and squatted down beside the small blue-eyed boy.

"Peter Brownhouse," the young boy said. "But don't tell them." He motioned his head toward the two women. "They think I'm a Comanche."

Reyas laughed and grinned. "You got them fooled?" he asked the boy confidentially.

"Yes," the boy said, and nodded in firm agreement.

"Would you go to my ranch with me?"

"Yes, sir, and you could find my paw for me?"

"I would try, Peter. Where is he?"

"I don't rightly know, but you can find him."

"I will, Peter, I will try." Reyas rose to his feet and spoke under his breath to Slocum. "Black Horn did not offer us the blue-eyed woman, did he?"

"No," Slocum said softly. "He is not through torturing her."

"Perhaps that is so. You can see these Comanche have very few children of their own. I don't know why, but others have pointed it out to me. One, maybe two per woman. That one woman eating bread yesterday had three, but they were half grown and she was not pregnant. They treasure a pregnant woman. They hope that she will have another warrior. That's what they want from these two little boys. More warriors."

"What will he ask for them?" Slocum asked, cupping an elbow in his hand and studying the northern horizon.

"If I am lucky, some bolts of cloth." Reyas then spoke to the two women and told them in Spanish they could take the children back. When they headed for the camp with their wards, he and Slocum strode away.

"Sometimes silver bits, no telling what he will ask. But the price will be stiff."

"Can you meet it?"

"I will try. Texans are generous. If I find one parent or a family that one of these poor babies belongs to, they will pay me enough to cover my costs for the rest."

"It doesn't get old for you, does it?" Slocum asked.

"What is that?"

"Saving such little kids from these red-assed savages."

"Hush, amigo. I am one of those bloodthirsty Comancheros. You will ruin my reputation among the gringos." Then Reyas chuckled.

"Someone needs to ruin it," Slocum said. He walked off to see about their horses. He needed some escape. Those pitiful children were caught as pawns in a dangerous game between these restless nomads and his own people, who planned to send these restless nomads to farmland. Bathless horseback heathens who only knew how to hunt buffalo, kill their enemy, then rape their enemy's wives, and take their sons captive for more braves. And General Sherman planned to make them tillers of the soil. Gawd. And the blue-eyed woman, Sug, haunted him too.

A wave of revulsion shook him.

6

Vin licked his cracked lips. On his belly in the short stiff grass, he had observed the hillside soddy for some time. A thin woman came out and hung some clothes on the line stretched from the upright wagon tongue to a nail over the door facing. Her laundry flapped noisily in the strong wind.

She was alone. Her man was nowhere in sight. Good. How many guns would she have? As long as she had a repeater, that was all he was concerned about.

Not much talk about Injuns attacking lately. Most of these sodbusters left their guns at the house. Better get on with his plan. No need to wait till her old man got back. He set out in a low run, coming in on the back side so she wouldn't see him until he was on her.

He eased himself down the slope and slipped along the face of the steep hillside, edging toward the open door. His hand was on the butt of his skinning knife. He would have to use it on her. He couldn't leave any witnesses so they'd think an Injun had done it. How many guns did she have?

His heart beat hard under his chest. Warily, he checked the rolling prairie and saw nothing out there, then sprang through the doorway. Her terrified cry met him as his eyes sought to adjust to the darkness of the room.

"Who are you?" she screamed, and her thin face blanched flour white.

"Hush your damn mouth," he said, looking around. Then he spied the repeater leaned beside the door beside him. He could make out the brass action, and felt relieved that she had what he needed. He turned back and slowly smiled at her.

She tried to dart past him. But he caught her and they struggled. They fell on the floor, and he managed to get on top of her and pin her facedown as he drew his knife. Twice he stabbed her in the side. Her screams hurt his eardrums. Soon blood ran from her wounds as he looked up and searched for something else to use on her.

He had to stop her screaming. He covered her mouth with his free hand. That shut off some of her yelling. This was a mess. He dropped the knife on the floor, and released her mouth in his frantic need to find a club to use. Her desperate cries for help began again.

"Gawd! Save me, someone !" she shouted. "I'm dying!"

Half holding her down with his knee in her back, he reached out and drew up a singletree lying beside the wall. *No one's going to save you.* He raised the singletree up over his head and swung it at her. Three good blows with it and he'd silenced her screaming. She lay facedown.

He rose, shaken, then swallowing hard with resolve, bent over to scalp her. He had to make it look like Injuns had done all this to her. He sawed with his sharp knife, scraping over her skull until a large patch of her hair came loose in his other hand. With the knife back in his sheath, he untangled his fingers from the hair and let it drop to the floor. With a deep sigh, he dropped to his knees, rolled her over, and ripped open the dress. He fought the garment off her limp form, and then removed her scant underclothing. Soon the stark white body with the small dried-up breasts, her belly crimsoned from the wounds, lay spread-eagled on the dirt floor. It would look like some bucks had raped her too.

He wadded up her clothing to take with him, wiping the

fresh blood from his hands on it. With the garments in a ball under his arm, he picked up the scalp, the good rifle, and a new cartridge-fitted Colt revolver in a holster that hung from the ladder-back chair. Some old buck would pay a lot for the pistol too, if they really wanted arms. For a moment, he considered setting the dugout on fire, but decided that the smoke might bring aid too fast. He rushed over and swept everything off the dry sink with the rifle barrel. His actions shattered the china dishes when they hit the floor. He needed for it to look like some savages had been there.

He stuck his head outside in the brilliant sunshine, his eyes adjusting to the brightness. Nothing in sight. He left on the run with the gunbelt slung over his shoulder and the ball of her clothing under his elbow. The precious Winchester was in his right hand.

When he reached the wash where the squaw held Clunny and the Indian pony that he'd bought for her, she jumped up from where she sat on the ground. He motioned for her to mount, and they rode west in a long trot. Along the way, he stopped and stuffed the woman's scalp and clothing in an old badger hole.

Six rifles, counting the one Spencer he traded for, was not enough to bring the chief. He needed a large number of rifles. Say, a crate or two of them.

They turned the horses loose to graze and went back to the shack that the squaw claimed at the edge of Ft. Dodge's settlement. It clouded up and rained that afternoon. Long streaks of silver lightning danced across the dark sky. Vin put on his canvas slicker to go see what he could learn about things around the fort. He needed to check out some of the camps of fresh arrivals. So he left her and hiked up the slick mud tracks.

He hesitated at a large tent near some newly arrived freight wagons. The smell of real wood smoke coming from the tin chimney tickled his nose. A thin bearded man standing in the opening waved him inside under the roof. It was a generous structure, with a row of six poles down the center and head high at the canvas sidewalls, with poles supporting it too. He walked through the horse gear stowed about on the floor, and headed for a sheet-iron stove in the center.

A gray-haired man held up a coffeepot, and Vin nodded, grateful for his offer. Some hot coffee would go good. He felt chilled under his canvas coat.

"Name's Punkin, that's Sedge," the older man said, motioning to the man who'd invited him in.

"Vin's my name."

"Sit a spell, Vin." Sedge motioned for him to squat down with him.

Outside, thunder rolled across the sky like loose potatoes in an empty wagon. A gust of hard wind and rain challenged the tent. Vin joined them on the ground.

"Thanks. You fellas freighters?" he asked, squatting on his boot heels. His socks were already soaked with water. It squashed inside his boots when he flexed his toes.

"Sort of," Sedge said, and held his hands out for the heat from the stove.

"Guess you're here to haul back some hides to St. Louie?"

"After a couple of us go down to Ft. Supply and deliver some repeaters and other stuff to a store down there."

"Some fellas buying repeaters in Ft. Supply?"

"Yeah, Gilbert's Mercantile. Them officers like to carry them, better than those muzzle-loading carbines the army issues them. Course they've got to buy 'em for themselves, so the post store sell lots of them. Buffalo hunters wouldn't have one. They ain't powerful enough for them."

"So—" His mind raced over this new information. Those damn officers didn't need those guns half as bad as he did. How could he get his hands on them? There had to be a way. He tried to clear his brain.

Squatted on his heels, he sipped their hot, fresh-tasting coffee and wondered. Killing damned old sodbusters' wives one at a time would never get him enough rifles in a lifetime to make him rich, but if he could get his hands on a lot of them, it would be a different story. He had to restrain himself so the two men didn't know his true purpose.

Then an idea struck him. What if he offered to deliver those guns to Ft. Supply? The two men could get to loading hides right away, and head back for the bright lights of St. Louis a lot sooner. At the very thought of St. Louis and having another belly ride on one of those creamy fat whores back there, he wanted to squeeze his scrotum.

Be plenty of time for all that later—when he was rich as one of those railroad tycoons, like Fitch or Gould. He'd heard of some of those millionaires lighting their cigars with banknotes.

"What would you pay for me to deliver them goods to Ft. Supply? I got me a wagon and could use some work."

"You'd have to ask Arney. He'll be back directly. But he'd sure pay you to do that, I'd bet," Punkin said, sounding interested.

"Yeah," Sedge said. "Sooner we get them stinking hides loaded and headed back home, the happier I'll be. Just thinking about damn Injuns out here makes my scalp itch."

"Hey, any you fellas got a horse to ride?" a man asked, sticking his dripping felt hat in the tent.

"No," came the chorus. "What's wrong?"

"We're going looking for a war party. They attacked some sodbuster's place, raped his poor wife and killed her."

"When?" Vin asked.

"Yesterday—I guess. He found her dead, scalped, and his place ransacked."

"What's the army doing about it?" Sedge asked.

"Same as always. They got patrols out." The man shrugged.

Over the drum of rain on the tent, Vin could hear other horses and riders outside. Things were working too good. The notion that he might soon have all the weapons he needed warmed him. He sipped more of the hot coffee.

7

"Not enough!" Black Horn screamed at Reyas. His face filled with rage, the chief jumped to his feet. In an awkward rambling gait, he paced back and forth beyond the spread-out blanket loaded with the trade goods that comprised Reyas's generous offer for the four children. Sunlight danced off the gold coins hung around Black Horn's neck, and the bells on his knee-high boots made a ringing accompaniment to his steps.

"They worth lot more!" Black Horn demanded. "You offer me nothing!"

"A dozen warm blankets. Six bolts of fine cloth. Six silver bits." Reyas pointed to his trade goods on the blanket. "There are matches to start your fire, tobacco to smoke. A dozen tins of peaches. Dried apples. Brown sugar and a stack of bread loaves."

Slocum stood back, his arms folded, and surveyed the two men's negotiations. Obviously the Comanche wanted a lot more for his young captives. Reyas showed patience, and acted undisturbed by the entire matter. If the chief wanted that much for the four children, Slocum wondered what he would ask for Sugar. A king's ransom, no doubt.

On the other hand, who else could Black Horn sell these

44

captives to? The number of Comancheros that would manage to slip by the army and come out here would be small this summer. At one time the trade of Comanche slaves and captives had been fierce on the New Mexico border. Great fleets of *caritas* coming from the Espanola Valley made their way out on the plains to deal with the Iteha. U.S. policy toward the hostiles had changed all that. Selling humans was no longer approved either, despite the centuries of such commerce in the Southwest.

"What more would you ask for them?" Reyas asked.

Black Horn stopped his pacing. His eyes like pinpoints of polished coal, he stared at Reyas as if weighing his options. At last he spoke. "All of this and the red horse you ride."

"The four children and the blue-eyed white woman captive," Reyas said back to him. "I will trade the red horse and all of this for them."

"I do not wish to trade her."

"I do not wish to trade the red horse, except for her and the children." The man acted as if that would be his final offer.

"I would trade her for ten rifles."

Reyas shook his head. "I have no rifles but my own."

Slocum listened. The price for Sugar's release was set. Black Horn would trade her—but only for ten rifles. And no doubt, they needed to be repeaters. He was only nine short of having that many. Not only that, he realized, looking across the vast sea of sweeping brown grass, there wasn't a place close by where he could get the other guns either.

"No trade for this." Black Horn abruptly turned on his heel and started for the camp.

Neither Slocum nor Reyas said a word while watching his retreat. The angry Comanche headed for the two women on their hands and knees, working on a large robe. Black Horn came up from behind and caught sugar unaware, snatching her up by the hair on her head. Slocum's hand went for his gun butt.

"Easy, *mi amigo*," Reyas said under his breath. "He does it to test our concern for her. Come, let us go behind the *caritas*. There is nothing we can do to stop him. Our concern for her will only make him feel more powerful when he comes back to trade again."

Slocum took his hand off the Colt. Slowly he dried his wet palm on his pants. He glanced over in time to see Black Horn savagely force his dick into Sugar's mouth. Filled with raw anger, Slocum followed the shorter man to the carts, and they went around behind them to be out of sight.

"Would you have traded him the red horse?" Slocum asked once they were out of sight.

Without turning, Reyas gave a nod. "He is only a horse. I can buy more or raise them. But a human's life is different—they have a soul."

Filled with a burning rage, Slocum drew in a shuddering breath. *You son of a bitch—someday I'll kill you for her.*

Reyas matter-of-factly promised Slocum that the chief would be back. However, Black Horn did not return again that day to negotiate. Slocum sat cross-legged on the ground under a wagon in the shade and studied the smoke-veiled Comanche camp. A new Winchester was across his lap. A million schemes to free the woman ran through his mind. None that were feasible enough to try came to him.

He bent over to look out when Reyas joined him and stood beside the rig, obviously watching the Comanches. "He sent word with a woman that he is moving in the morning," said Reyas.

"Is he testing you?" Slocum asked, tossing small pinches of dry grass up for the wind to carry away.

"He is not one of the chiefs that I like to trade with, but we are here."

Slocum's gaze fell to the rifle in his lap. "What will you do?"

"I will offer the same things and some more."

"The red horse?"

Reyas dropped to his haunches. "If I have to. Yes, even the horse. Those children would be on my mind if I did not try to save them."

8

The boss of the freighter frowned at Vin. "How much do you want to take that freight to Ft. Supply?"

"What'll you pay?" Vin asked to sound cagey. The old man would become suspicious if he didn't dicker some with him about the money he wanted.

"Not a dime more than I have to."

"Say forty bucks?"

Arney shook his head, and held out his stained cup for Sedge to pour him more coffee. "But I'd consider thirty."

"Thirty-five, if it's less than five hundred pounds."

"Be more like seven hundred."

"I could haul that." Hell, he could haul it if he needed to buy another mule and a new wagon.

"It's robbery, too much money. But I'll pay it to get headed back home that much quicker." Arney took a sip of his coffee. "You ever been to Ft. Supply?"

"Yeah, I can get there."

"Guess anyone could if they wanted to bad enough."

"Take me four or five days."

"Yeah, I figured that. Bring your rig over in the morning and we'll put on the freight goes down there."

"Good enough." Vin stuck out his hand, gave the man a

48

Masonic handshake, then met his gaze and both nodded.

"Nice to know you're one of us," Arney said, and Vin excused himself, promising to be back at first light. He would never forget the grateful looks of those other freighters when he waved good-bye to them. He'd saved them from going all the way to Ft. Supply down in the Indian Nation. Good thing he'd learned that Masonic handshake from old Bucky Drain when they were in the guardhouse together. It worked every time he used it.

He hurried back to the shack. When he returned, the squaw was gone. He took a seat on the floor, discovering that rainwater had seeped in and her blanket was wet. He hung it on a nail on the wall to dry, and fixed some crate boards into a bench. Where had she gone? Strange, he thought, listening to the drip of rain off the eaves, she had never left before.

At last, he put his canvas coat on and decided to go look for her. The rain had a chill, and he wished for a fire to warm by as he stepped out into the dismal downpour. He went by the scales shed first, and talked to the old man who watched things.

"You seen my squaw?" Vin asked him when he crowded inside the building past where the old man sat in a rocker to view the yard.

The man spat a big brown gob of tobacco out the open door. "I ain't seen a damn thing."

Vin shrugged off the toothless bastard's snotty ways. The man had been sitting there too long guarding a couple of mountains of hairy hides.

"Thanks." Vin went back out in the driving rain. Where else could he look for her? In the town? He hurried in that direction. Strange for her to run off. They had food and supplies left at the shack. Where could she be? Damn, he needed her to take him to this chief Black Horn. No way would he ever be able to find him without her. He grew edgy, and walked faster in the deluge. It was soaking through the canvas and wetting his shirt. His boots were full of water as if he'd waded a stream.

He entered the first bar and bought a drink. He knew the barkeep's name was Davies. "You seen a squaw in a white girl's dress tonight?"

"Naw. You seen one in here tonight?" Davies asked the tall man next to Vin.

"I ain't," the man said, and hoisted his beer for a swig.

Vin downed the shot of whiskey he'd ordered and paid the man. The liquor warmed him going down and he felt better, but her disappearance had begun to niggle him more inside. He needed to find her.

At the next bar, no one had seen a squaw either. A couple of the hunters gave him big horse laughs about how if they'd seen her they'd damn sure not have shared her with him. Vin moved on. Only the two stores and one more bar to check.

He stopped in the downpour when he heard something.

"Come on, Injun gal, take you another big drink."

His anger turned to full rage when he looked between two tents and saw this big fella in wet buckskins feeding whiskey to his squaw. The new dress was so wet it clung to her. Her short hair was plastered to her skull, and she looked pitifully small.

"Get the hell away from her!" Vin shouted.

"Who in the fuck are you?"

"That's my woman!"

"She ain't got no brand on her ass. She and I were having us a friendly drinking game here."

"Come on!" Vin shouted, holding out his hand for her. She looked at it, then, as if she dared him, raised the brown bottle to take another drink.

"See there, she don't want to have nothing to do with you," the buckskinner said.

"Keep out of this!" Vin warned. "Come on, girl, we're going to our place."

"You ain't going nowhere with her." The buckskinner

swung a huge Arkansas toothpick at Vin, who bolted back barely in time to escape the tip of the shiny point. When the man missed, the keen edge sliced into the nearby tent wall and ripped a place where the yellow light could seep out.

Vin managed to haul out his Colt as he stepped backward. He drove the muzzle forward and cocked the hammer, and the gun went off in a cloud of acrid smoke. The buckskinner dropped his knife and bent over, obviously hit, but Vin had no idea where. He savagely clubbed the man on the head with the gun butt, and sent him facedown into the mud. The crowds in the two nearby saloons were shouting and fixing to emerge.

He grabbed her by the wrist and rushed off the back way. They almost slipped in the mud going around the corner. Three men coming out the back flap of the White Elephant saw him and his gun; they drove back inside, yelling, "Take cover!"

She matched his speed, and they ran through the hide yards, drawing some watchdogs' barks. Out of breath, Vin glanced back, wondering if anyone was on their trail, but saw no pursuit in the slanting rain.

He shoved her in the door of the shack, and once on the inside searched for something to whip her with. His short breath whistled through his throat. She'd learn not to run off on him. From his saddle he took the bridle and began lashing her across the butt with the reins. She danced around the small room with him in pursuit. He caught her butt with the reins every few swings, until they both collapsed out of breath.

He leaned his face against the rough lumber and strained for air. She clung to some crates and heaved to recover her wind.

"You run off again, I'll cut your nose off." He made a slicing motion at his own face. "You understand?"

She nodded. The bitch knew English. She knew what he

meant. He'd treat her like a Comanche would if she ever ran off again on him.

He listened to the thunder rumble across the sky. He still had lots of work to do. Cold drops of rain leaked in and dripped on his back. The drum of the rain continued. Helluva summer storm, was all he could think. Would the buckskinner show up again, or had he killed him? No way to know. He'd best make tracks out of Ft. Dodge early, in case that sumbitch had friends that wanted to even the score.

He fitted her with a canvas poncho and took her with him when he went to find the mule, Jacob. They located the large black animal grazing with a loose mare near the river. He looked at the rain-splattered brown water with some dread, then turned back to his task of capturing the mule. After running this way and that to prevent Jacob's escape, they cornered him and at last led him back to the shack.

"We're going to tie him up," Vin announced. "I want him close by come sunup. We're going to go find Black Horn. You savvy Black Horn?"

She nodded. Then she raised her arm under the canvas poncho and pointed south.

"Yeah, we're heading for Ft. Supply, only we really ain't going there." No need to explain much to her anyway. The fact that he was going to get the damn rifles given to him made him giddy enough that his stomach churned at the prospect.

It was a gray sunup, but there was no rain. Vin had the two horses hitched to the back of his wagon, their gear inside the box. With Jacob in the shafts and Vin and the squaw on the spring seat, they headed for the wagon train. He was grateful he didn't need to drive into town, for fear of more trouble from the night before. Soon he reined up at the freighters' camp.

"This all goes Gilbert's Mercantile down there," Arney

said as the others began to bring out the crates containing the rifles.

"I understand. You got any papers?"

"Yeah, in here, just give them to the man. He'll know. They're dry, so don't get them wet." Arney handed him a packet in oilskin, and Vin shoved it inside his shirt.

"He going to pay me, or you?"

"Hold your damn horses. I will." Arney dug out a double eagle to give him, and then counted out fifteen silver dollars. "You be certain you get there with this freight."

"Take me a few days—maybe three, I figure with only one mule—but I'll get there."

"What's your name again?"

"Vin Malloy."

Arney nodded. "Put one of our wagon sheets over them and tie it down too," he said to his men, motioning to the crates. He turned back to Vin and scowled. "I hate the prospect of hauling them stinking old green hides back. Wagons will stink like that forever. But we need to get back. You taking the ferry across the river?"

"I better," Vin agreed, unhappy about paying the fifty-cent toll. Still, he needed his precious cargo to survive. The night before he had gathered all the other weapons from the various hiding places, and now had them wrapped in blankets under his saddle and gear.

"See you again sometime, Malloy," Arney said, and the other freighters gave him a good-bye wave.

Vin clucked to Jacob and the mule settled into the collar. He eased the wagon forward, and soon had the load moving. Rather than go into the settlement, Vin swung the mule southward and headed for the ferry.

He arrived at the river, and the operator came out of the tent.

"Stirring early, ain't you, mister?"

"Got to get this to Ft. Supply." Vin nodded toward his load.

"I guess we can cross. River came up some more last

night." The man straightened his suspenders and spat tobacco to the side.

"I need to be on my way."

"You in town last night?"

"Nope," Vin lied.

"They shot some fella."

"Who?"

"I didn't get many details, but the one they shot was an ex-army scout by the name of Sam Durant."

"Kill him?"

"They think he'll pull through. Bullet caught him under the armpit and went through him."

"He's lucky," Vin said, and clucked for Jacob to get on the ferry's board surface. It took a few tries, but at last, the obstinate mule pulled the wagon on board, and the two horses were tied at the side for the crossing.

The ferryman undid the lines and stepped to the crank. He began to rewind the rope that stretched from shore to shore and unwind the other end. A protesting creak of the spools, and then the barge began to move. Muddy water slapped the upstream side of the barge.

Vin stood beside the wagon. He could hardly believe that the whole thing had gone so smoothly. He had the guns to sell to the chief. Plenty of them, if he could find this Black Horn—actually, if she could lead him to his camp. All he had to worry about was if the chief still had his express box full of money to pay him. What if someone else had beaten him there and already gotten all the money?

He looked at the large sag in the ferry's rope as they approached midstream. The force of the river's current was making the bank-to-bank cable form a great bow.

"Hey," he shouted to the operator. "Is that rope going to hold us?"

"It should." The man looked up and blinked in disbelief at the state of the tow rope. He began to crank faster.

9

Reyas stood in the gray light of dawn. Some fast-moving clouds were passing through the sky. Beside the man, Slocum rubbed his bristled mouth on the side of his hand, and they both watched the Comanches break camp. There were excited barking dogs, stallions screaming challenges, squaws talking and giving orders as tepee sides were lowered. Boys in their teens on horseback had the loose horses not needed to haul things in a herd moving to the south. The plaintive rasping sound of a braying stud jack rose above the rest of the camp sounds.

"It sure don't look like he wants to trade with you," Slocum said.

"It may all be an act. He's a big actor."

"You know him well enough to suspect he will trade in the end?"

"He has to. There won't be many, if any, traders come to see him this summer. His supplies will get low. The extra things I offered him for the captives can be gifts at a later time to settle the squaws."

"You think those poor women have that much influence on him?"

"They do." Reyas turned and smiled confidently at him.

Slocum shook his head and went for some more coffee. The past twenty-four hours had been filled with disappointment for him. He'd first thought the chief would accept Reyas's goods for the children. Perhaps Black Horn didn't know the seriousness of the army's embargo on trade with the Comanches.

"Where will we go next?" Slocum asked.

"Go up to the Canadian River. There are Cheyenne around there who should be ready to trade."

"Where is this big canyon I have heard about?" Slocum asked.

"It is to the south, maybe a hundred miles from here. It is where many of these tribes winter."

Slocum nodded. Still no sign that Black Horn would change his mind. Time seeped away. Already, many of the lodge poles were down and being tied to horses to haul. Smoke still swirled around the camp from the remains of the fires.

The cook, Jiminez, nodded to Slocum and used a doubled-up kerchief on the metal handle of the coffeepot to pour Slocum's tin cup full. He set the large pot back on the grate.

"The Comanches are ignoring us," the gray-headed man said.

"Yes," Slocum agreed, and raised his cup to blow away the steam.

"They know we're here and ready to ransom those poor children."

"The chief is the one," Slocum said, thinking about Sug's mistreatment at his hands. "He's showing his power."

"*Sí.* I hope his big-dicked horse bucks him off on a cactus."

Slocum grinned as the older man busied himself with his cooking, muttering away, "I hate those Comanches. I always swear I am never coming back here, and then that Don Reyas comes and says, 'Oh, Jiminez, I need you so badly.' " The man shook his head in disgust. "And I come again."

Slocum smiled, and moved back to where Reyas was seated on a blanket.

"We will move eastward up the Canadian," Reyas said.

"How far away are the Kiowa?" Slocum asked.

"We could find them too. All three tribes are sharing this last large area for the great buffalo herd. At one time they were all enemies, the Comanche, Kiowa, and Cheyenne, but now they have to get along. Can't afford to fight among themselves with the whites pressuring them so hard."

Slocum nodded. The last of the tepee poles were down, and the band spread over the prairie as they all went off. The horse herd was already gone from sight. Women and children with the loaded horses were all that he and Reyas had left to watch.

"Load up the train, Juarez," Reyas said to his man. "We will go to the old fort."

"Bent's old trading post?" Slocum asked.

"Yes, the old one, where Carson attacked these tribes during the war. No much left there. Have you been there before?"

"Once. I spent a night there passing through."

"You were a very brave man to come down through there alone. That is in the heart of the Indians' hunting grounds and there's usually several bands in that area."

Slocum shrugged. The best he could recall, there'd been two bounty hunters on his tail when he'd left the Sante Fe Trail near Ft. Dodge. His passage through such hostile territory had not been planned. However, he'd managed to evade them somewhere along the way. Either they'd turned back or simply given up. He'd made his way unharmed from there back west, and eventually into the San Juan Mountains of New Mexico. In fact, he'd only seen a few of the Indian camps from a great distance, and luckily had never met a war party or hunting party in his hurried crossing.

"Colonel Carson had two small cannons he used there, they say," Reyas said. "Carson, with his Home Guard and the California Volunteers, shelled some of the nearby villages camped there along the river for the winter. The Indians ran one way, and Carson was low on supplies by then, so he went back home to Taos. Was not a big battle. Hardly even fazed the Indians. But at the time, everyone else was back East fighting too."

Slocum nodded. He had met the small man one time in Taos. He'd expected a huge grizzly bear of a person, and the mild-mannered Carson, short and slight as a boy, was hardly what he had envisioned from the stories that had been related to him.

"If I had bet with you that Black Horn would trade with us, I would have lost," Reyas said, picking up the black-and-white-patterned blanket he had sat upon and shaking out the dry grass from it.

"Black Horn has other things on his mind. He's determined to get those rifles at any cost."

Reyas agreed, then shook his head in disgust. "God forbid that he does."

In an hour, the screeching *carita* axles again sounded like a lot of out-of-tune bagpipes. A small cloud of dust rose over the train as the oxen plodded to the northeast in a great chain of the rigs. Slocum and Reyas rode to the side, and could survey the snakelike progress of the line.

"There is a large spring ahead where we can camp tonight," Reyas said. "If there is no tribe staying there."

"Good," Slocum said. He wondered how to prepare himself for his return to rescue Sugar. He'd promised he would come back—no matter the consequences. It would be tough—tough to find the Comanches again and tough not to lose his scalp to some other savages in the process.

Near sundown, they made camp at the spring. Slocum had ridden in a great circle to make sure they were not near another unseen encampment. The twilight was past when he returned to camp, speaking softly to the night guard when he rode past him.

Somewhere out in the night, a buffalo wolf howled, and another returned his lonesome throaty cry. Their chilling voices carried across the open prairie in a solemn song. Slocum checked the stars as he squatted down at the cooking fire.

"You are late, Señor," Jiminez said, and showed him the snowy flour tortillas in the closed Dutch oven and pointed to the fire-browned meat on the grill. "There are frijoles in that one and peppers in here."

"*Gracias, amigo,*" he said, and began to fill his tin plate. Reyas joined him where he sat cross-legged on the ground.

"Nothing out there," Slocum said between bites, realizing how hungry he was. The browned buffalo steak tasted good. Jiminez brought him steaming coffee.

"Good. We can reach the Canadian in two days," Reyas said. "If we make a good trade there with some of those bands we can head for home—say, in a week. Is that soon enough for you?"

"You're paying the bills," Slocum said.

"Juarez told me that white woman came to you for help. I know that you are anxious to return for her."

"I made a deal with you."

"I am pleased you are a man of your word. I was sorry I could not trade for her."

"I hate that the children could not be rescued as well."

The campfire light reflecting from his face, Reyas nodded slowly. "It was a very depressing time we spent with Black Horn."

"He needs to be sent to his reward," Slocum said, swabbing up the bean juices on the plate with the tortilla.

"Now where would that be?" Reyas asked, amused. "Sleep well tonight, Juarez has enough guards."

Slocum nodded. The food was fast making him sleepy. A good night's rest, if he could sleep, might be the answer for him. He chewed on the strip of rich-tasting roasted meat.

Hours later, he awoke from deep slumber. He heard a commotion at the edge of camp. It was the first night in a while that he had had such deep sleep. He had slept very lightly near the Comanches, waking to every faint dog's bark in their camp.

"What is it?" he asked an armed guard rushing by him.

"Someone on horseback coming in," he said over his shoulder.

Slocum sat up and quickly pulled on his boots, then hitched on his gunbelt as he hurried to see what was happening. It was difficult for him to completely awaken. Where was Reyas? He reached the dark knot of guards and a horse.

"Who is it?" he asked over their Spanish talk.

"Me! Sug Irons. That you?" she asked, sounding excited.

"How in the hell did you—"

"Got up and left that gawdamn place, that's how. Your name's?" Even in the starlight he could see her look hard at him for his answer.

"Slocum," he said as she came through the men.

"Good. I'm here now."

"What about Black Horn?"

"I really don't give a big gawdamn. I'm rid of him."

"What is happening?" Reyas asked, joining them.

"Blue Eyes left the Comanches tonight. Don Reyas, meet Sugar Irons."

"Good evening, Señorita. Have you had any food?"

"No, but I could eat some."

"Come," he said, extending his arm to her as if she were some belle of the ball.

She gave Slocum a raised eyebrow, then took Reyas's arm. "I'm with you," she said as the man led her to the cook's camp.

Slocum told them he would join them later. He walked

over and under the starlight, studied the lathered, hard-breathing horse she'd ridden in on. Not one of Black Horn's prize stallions anyway. He might think another buck had taken her—no, he would come looking for her. It would be a thing he could not resist doing. Her presence could endanger the entire train. No telling how many bands Black Horn could arouse and gather up to join him.

Slocum nodded to the youth who was ready to lead the pony away. He'd better go talk to Sugar and Don Reyas. There was a lot at stake with her there. It would all need to be thought out. Damn, here he had been concerned about how to rescue her, and she'd simply ridden away.

"So you have no one to return to?" Reyas asked her as Slocum joined them.

"No. I can't go back to Texas." She shook her head. Her raggedly cut short hair shone with bear grease in the firelight.

Slocum nodded to them and eased himself to the ground close by.

"She says she can't go home," Reyas said to him.

"I heard her. How soon you figure Black Horn will be coming after her?"

She blinked at Slocum in the orange light. "You think—"

Reyas slowly nodded. "I think he will come for her. It will be a slap in his face for a woman to leave him. Especially a white woman."

"Wh-what does that mean?" she asked, wildly searching their faces. "You're going to give me back to him?"

"No, but we may need to send you somewhere safe," said Slocum.

"Where would that be?" She stopped eating and waited for an answer.

"There is Ft. Supply north of here," Reyas said to him. "There are soldiers there."

"How far away?" Slocum asked.

"Eighty miles perhaps, maybe more."

"How would we get her there?"

"You would have to take her," Reyas said.

"But your safety?"

The man shrugged as if unconcerned. "You are a good man, amigo, but I have been doing this since I was a boy. Juarez and the others will protect me."

"I made you a promise."

"You have kept it. I will miss your company. Of course, I will pay you."

"It isn't the money." Slocum shook his head.

"Take some fresh horses and you can be there in two days. Once she is safe—or perhaps take her on to Ft. Dodge—then she can get a wagon ride east or west on the Sante Fe Trail."

Slocum inhaled deeply and considered the notion. He wanted her safe, but not at the price of Don Reyas's life. His gut instinct told him the man would be vulnerable without him. Why he worried, he couldn't say, but he hated to go against his gut feelings. His intuition had proven right nine out of ten times.

"You think he'll come after me?" she asked.

"Oh, he will," Reyas said.

"I'll ride on. No need to mess up you-all's lives. I'm the one that he wants. I'll go by myself. You tell me how to get there."

"No. Slocum will take you there. Do you need more food?"

"Maybe some more meat." She started to rise, but Reyas made her stay and went for it himself.

"I'll get some horses ready," Slocum said.

"Stay seated," Reyas said, and whistled.

Juarez soon came over and squatted down beside the man. He nodded at Reyas's orders.

"I am giving her the bay to ride," Reyas said.

Slocum nodded. "I don't need Eagle. I can ride another."

"No, amigo, you must ride the best. Those two could outrun most Indian mustangs should you need fleet ones. Besides, I want you to come and visit my ranch when this is over. We will drink some fine wine and listen to the music—in peace, I hope."

"Can I ask a big favor?" she said between bites on the strip of meat.

"Yes?"

"I want a pair of man's pants and a man's shirt to wear. The sooner I can get out of these stinking rags the better."

"You wish to change now?" Reyas asked.

"No." She shook her head with her mouth full and finished chewing. "After I take a bath, I can put them on."

"Jiminez, go find a boy's britches and a shirt for her. Oh, and a sombrero. The sun will be bright out there."

"You are much too generous," she said.

"If I had a daughter, I would only hope someone else would look out for her."

Slocum watched her bite her lower lip to fight back the tears. Eventually she suppressed them, and nodded at Reyas with a hard swallow that even hurt him.

Juarez's boys soon brought both animals saddled and ready. Slocum noticed that even his bedroll was tied on behind his saddle. The cook handed Sugar the clothing in a burlap sack to tie on the horn, and she flopped the hat on that he gave her, then drew up the chin string.

"How will I ever repay you?" she asked Reyas.

"By living a good life. You will find one. May God help you—" Then she rushed over and kissed him. Her action sent his sombrero off his head, and for a moment, he looked taken aback by her show of emotion.

He patted her on the arms, then came over to Slocum with a small leather pouch. "Here is your money. Come see me when you are in the valley."

"*Gracias.*" Slocum shook his firm hand, then tucked the money inside his shirt. "I will be by to see you."

"I am counting on it. Don't let them take your scalp," Reyas said with a laugh.

Slocum, in the saddle, nodded. "I'll damn sure try not to let them." He turned to Sugar. "You ready?"

Seated in the saddle, she nodded.

With the North Star to guide them, they rode out of camp in a long trot. Slocum intended to be many miles beyond Black Horn's grasp by sunup. On the last rise, he looked back and could see the small flicker of the campfire. He turned the gray into the night wind, and without any words they rode on.

At dawn, they reached the Canadian. The silver water rushed along under the cottonwoods and willows. She dropped from the bay and handed him the reins.

"You have any soap?" she asked.

"I think so," he said, and twisted in the saddle to reach in his bags.

When he turned back, she was already out of the filthy rag dress. He blinked at her shapely stark white form, the long shapely breasts capped with pink nipples. No wonder Black Horn had chosen her.

"Here," he said.

"Sorry, guess I don't have any morals left. But I wore them stinking clothes as long as I was going to."

"Don't blame you." He handed her the soap and swung down.

The first rays of a golden dawn lanced across the sky. They dazzled in reds and yellows on the rushing water as she waded out into it. Then without concern, she began to lather herself and rinse the soap away. At last, seated on the bottom, she soaped the long ivory stems of her legs with the tanned feet. Her dark brown face, arms, and hands were in contrast to the rest of her snowy skin.

He squatted on the bank. A bath looked inviting to him, but the urge for them to move on was stronger. They needed to be certain they were beyond Black Horn's grasp. Or the grasp of any other band as well. They were deep in the country of the southern herd of buffalo. Any direction they went, they might run into a bunch of Indians.

At last finished bathing, she waded toward him. He handed her a towel and looked away as she dried herself.

"You are a strong man," she said. "Why do you work for men like Reyas?"

"He pays well."

"No, you aren't a worker. When I saw you that day, I thought you owned that train of carts."

"I'm no businessman."

"Do you own a ranch, a mine—"

"I'm a fugitive. A man on the run. No home. No place to take my boots off."

"I see. But you have been a landowner?"

He shook his head. "Lost all that in the war."

"Others did too, and they rebuilt."

"There are things in my past that won't let me."

She buttoned the fresh shirt and then tied the bottom. With a pop, she shook out the pants and drew them on.

"I haven't been dressed like a boy since I was twelve. That was when Paw said, 'Put that girl in a dress before she forgets she is one. She can outrope her damn lazy brothers.' "

"You stop roping then?"

"No, I can still outrope them. But I had to wear a dress after that." She tugged on the waistband to pull the pants up. "They could have been bigger."

Slocum gave her an admiring glance and shook his head. "Fit looks good to me."

"You ever been told you have a mean way about you, Slocum?"

He looked up into her smiling face and shook his head. "Not me. We better get to riding."

"When will we be safe?"

"When we get to Ft. Supply, I guess."

"How much further is it?"

"By my calculations another sixty miles."

"We came about twenty is all?"

"That's my guess."

She gave him back his towel after drying her short ragged hair. "Sure be glad when it grows out some." Then she mounted up and they crossed the river.

He used some high points to stop and survey the country. To the east, he could see smoke. Probably camps of Cheyenne, Kiowa, or other Comanches that Reyas hoped to find. The camps lay south of the two travelers in the Canadian River bottoms. Satisfied there was no smoke in the north, they remounted and rode in a long trot in that direction.

He fed her some jerky and hard candy from his saddlebags. They sipped tepid canteen water, then pushed their horses until sundown. He found a spring-fed creek and stopped.

"I haven't seen a sign of anything. We can sleep here a few hours."

"That won't be hard," she said with a groan, and dropped heavily from the saddle.

His own horse unsaddled, he went to where she fumbled with the latigos. Her forehead was resting on the seat, and she looked about to pass out. He moved in and undid the bedroll the Mexicans had tied on for her. He unfurled it.

"I'll do the horses. Lay down," he said.

"I—I can do—my part. . . ."

"Do it." He moved her away from the horse and stripped out the leathers.

"You're bossy," she said, and fell to her knees. Then she plopped down on the bedroll, used her hands for a pillow, and closed her eyes. He grinned at her form as he hobbled the bay. She was already asleep.

When the horses were cared for, he made her get under the blankets. In a few hours, the heat of the day would evaporate and she'd be shivering before she awoke to the cold. Her only words were mumbled as she obeyed him, and he didn't bother to ask her if she wanted any supper.

His chores completed in the twilight, he took a fist of jerky and went to sit on the ridge above their camp. He wanted to make certain there was nothing out there to challenge them. Besides, he needed to let the tension of the hard ride evaporate. In another tough day's travel, they should find Ft. Supply, if they didn't ride by it and miss it.

10

Vin skirted west of Ft. Supply. He had not realized how close he came to driving straight into the outpost until it was almost too late to avoid it. Of course, with the crates tarped down, no one might have noticed, thinking he was some squaw man out buffalo hunting.

"Which way is this chief of yours?" he asked, taking a midday break. "He usually near the Canadian River?"

"Yes, river," she agreed with a nod.

"We better keep our eyes out for other tribes," Vin said out loud. They were past the military. He hoped some army patrol wouldn't stop him and demand to search the wagon. Then he would be in real trouble. But they might meet the wrong bunch of redskins out here as well, and the Injuns would simply take the guns away.

It was the first time he had real doubts about making this sale. Before, all he could think about was the money, and lots of it. But since they had skirted Ft. Supply, he wasn't half as sure as he had been in Ft. Dodge about making contact and selling those guns for all the money the squaw had promised him.

Late afternoon, driving south, he spotted a wagon with some grazing mules nearby that lifted their heads and brayed at his animals. Good, a buffalo hunters' camp. Be safe enough to camp close to them for a night.

"There's a camp ahead," he said to her.

Seated beside him, she nodded and clung to the seat's iron rod railing. The prairie was rough, and the tracks he followed were uneven and rocked the wagon a lot.

"Hello the camp!" Vin shouted.

A boy of perhaps fifteen in a stained apron appeared and waved them in with a large spoon.

"Be good to have some white folks to talk with," Vin said under his breath to her.

"Howdy, mister!" the boy said, still branishing the large wooden spoon when Vin pulled up short of his camp. The teen's eyes were on the squaw, widened in disbelief at the sight of her.

"She yours?" he asked.

"Yeah," Vin said as he tied off the reins and stepped down. "Your people out hunting?"

"Yeah, shooting and skinning 'em. I'm Malcolm Whitney."

"Vin Malloy. This here's Raven."

"That's her name?"

"That's the name I call her. That's all that matters. You got any coffee?"

The boy could hardly take his eyes off her. He waved at the pot on the campfire and nodded. "Yeah, help yourself."

"I will," Vin said, and wiped his runny nose on his coat sleeve. Damn rain had given him a cold. He hated summer colds. He found a tin cup and poured himself some coffee. When he looked up, the boy had the squaw backed against the wagon. He was talking a blue streak at her.

"She understand English?" the boy asked over his shoulder.

"Some. Let her take that mule loose and water him."

"Oh, can I help her?"

"I guess so. Take the horses too." Vin dropped to his haunches.

"We will. What tribe's she from?"

"Comanche." Hell, that boy hadn't been out West long. Anyone knew a ragged-ass-looking girl like her was a Comanche. The Cheyennes were the lookers.

"You ain't afraid she'll cut your throat?" the boy asked, undoing the mule's traces.

Vin shook his head. He was more afraid of her running off for some more liquor.

"Paw'll sure be surprised," the boy said as he and the girl took the mule and two horses toward the small stream.

"Bet he will be," Vin said, and sipped the bitter coffee. He watched them, considering what he should do next. If they were tough enough, he might hire the boy's paw and kin for backup. A few extra guns in his camp might beat going it alone to trade with this Black Horn. He'd have to look them over before he decided.

It was late in the afternoon when a tall man with a beard came riding a thin black horse into camp. He wore a plug hat that was frosted with red dust, and something had bitten a hunk out of the brim. With a wry scowl, the man nodded at Vin and dismounted, giving his rifle and reins to the boy.

"Prescott Whitney," the man said, and stuck out his hand.

"Vin Malloy. We was just resting here. Me and her. Going south a ways. Hunting good here?"

Whitney shook his head. "Stragglers are all we find. Got two today. My other sons are out there skinning them now. Never found the main herd since we've been down here."

"You see any Injun camps?"

"No. Some signs of where they'd been. They told us at Ft. Supply most of them were south of the Canadian. We're staying up here for now, so we don't mix up with them."

"Guess you and your boys don't need any work?"

"What kind?"

"Nothing hard. I'm going to do some trading with her chief." He motioned toward the squaw. "I figured a couple of hunters along might keep the chief from thinking about robbing me."

"You know him?"

Vin shook his head. "No, but she says I can trade with him."

Whitney looked hard at her, and then with a skeptical frown on his face, turned back. "You trust her?"

"Oh, yeah, I came this far. I could pay a hundred bucks for you and your boys' services."

"When they get back here, we'll talk it over."

"Fair enough."

"What're you trading them?"

"Usual geegaws, beads and stuff for their hides."

"Be damn sight easier to trade for hides than kill and skin them," Whitney said, settling down on his haunches with his coffee cup as if he was considering the offer.

"Yeah, I've done both," Vin said.

It was near sundown when the two other Whitney boys rode in with a hide apiece over their laps. They were big strapping boys fresh out of their teens, and shook hands and introduced themselves as Collie and Grant. They too stared a lot at the squaw.

After a big meal of buffalo and beans, they sat around the low-burning chip fire and openly discussed Vin's offer.

"I'd sure try it," Grant said, and sliced off a hunk of the tobacco plug. He offered it around, then rewrapped it in oilskin and pocketed it when no one asked for any.

"You know where this one's at?" Collie asked. "The chief, I mean?"

"She'll take us to him."

"He camped around here?"

"She says south of here."

"You had her long?" Grant asked.

"A while. She knows where he's at. Don't worry. He wants to trade with me, so it shouldn't be nothing but a cut-and-dried deal. Like I told your paw, I just like to have some backing is all."

"I could understand that," Collie agreed, and the rest nodded around the campfire.

"Someone's coming," Malcolm said, and jumped to his feet.

Vin held out his hand to stay them. "Not a word to anyone about our deal. I don't want no one to beat me to this chief."

They quickly agreed, and rose to see who the intruder was. Vin brushed the dry grass off his butt and trailed after them. Just so it wasn't some nosy army scouts poking around. Who else could be out there? A lost hunter?

"Hello the camp," Slocum shouted, reining up the gray. Sugar held the bay back a few feet. No telling who was in the camp. If he didn't have her along, he wouldn't have been so slow to approach them.

"Come in, stranger," Prescott said.

"We saw the light of your fire," Slocum said.

"Both of you get down and rest a spell," Prescott said. "These here are my boys." And he named them. "That's Vin Malloy and his squaw."

"Slocum's my name, and this is Safra Irons."

"That a girl?" Grant asked in shock.

"Yes, a lady. She's been a captive of the Comanche. I'm taking her to Ft. Supply."

Prescott removed his plug hat and bowed. "I am most sorry, ma'am. Come, we have food and coffee."

"Thanks," she said after Slocum nodded that she should go with the man.

"What band had her?" Collie asked.

"Black Horn's."

"You seen him lately?" Vin asked.

"A few days ago. Why?"

"Oh, I just wondered. My squaw's from his band and she wants to go see her people."

Slocum nodded. That made sense. He took the coffee the boy offered, and noted they had gotten out a canvas folding chair for Sugar to sit upon. She looked embarrassed as they were all trying to serve her something.

The old man finally came over to where Slocum stood

and asked, "How long was the poor girl a captive?"

"Near a year, I guess. They took her last fall or winter under a full moon."

"She doesn't appear to be with child." Whitney frowned in the starlight.

"Ain't 'cause they didn't try. She's been severely abused."

"Oh, yes, I imagine so. Are you taking her back to her people?"

"No, she's going to New Mexico and live with a family there."

"Oh, how come?"

"She'd rather not go back. She has her reasons."

"I imagine so."

Slocum nodded to the man and went to refill his coffee cup. It was good to have some hot brew to drink—even the bitterness tasted all right. They had ridden hard all day, and he hoped to be in striking distance of Ft. Supply in another day. This camp of hide hunters acted civilized enough, and he wasn't particularly concerned for her safety. He had been among other hunters before who were wilder than savages.

He noted the two rigs. The tall wagon with bows and the other one, tarped down with "Arney Freight Lines, St. Louis, Mo." in big letters on the sheet. He took a plate of food and went to squat on his boot heels near Sugar.

"They ain't seen a white woman in ages," he said softly to her.

She pushed the sombrero back so it fell on her shoulders. "I could tell. But they act pleasant enough."

"No problem. That squaw comes from Black Horn's camp." Slocum nodded his head in her direction.

"Her name is Raven. She's one of Black Horn's wives."

"You know her?" he asked, looking around to see if the others were listening. Then he shook his head to silence her.

How in the hell did this Malloy get one of the Comanche

chief's women away from him? It didn't make sense. They'd best not say any more until he figured it out. He shook his head slightly to discourage her from talking any more about it. Soon the boys came over and engaged him by asking about whether he had seen any large buffalo herds. The conversation went on for some time.

After a while, he thanked them and excused himself and Sugar. He led the two horses out on the prairie a good distance from camp.

"Who is this Raven?" he asked, looking warily back at the starlit rigs on the pearl grassland.

"One of Black Horn's wives, like I said. She rode off from camp weeks ago. I thought it was funny then that he was not mad about her absence. Another of his wives, Blue Deer, left camp with a young warrior, and Black Horn trailed her for ten days. That is how Comanche women divorce their husbands—they leave with another man. He brought her back with two black eyes and kept her tied up for days."

"Did he send this Raven to bring back these white men?"

Sug shook her head. "I don't know, Slocum. But he never acted upset about her going away."

"I want to keep some distance away from their camp—in case—"

"In case of what?"

"In case there is something there about them and their connection to Black Horn."

"Fine," she said, and tightened her cinch.

Slocum adjusted his, and looked back at the wagon top in the starlight. Too many unanswered questions to suit him. But his prime responsibility was to get her to safety—somewhere that Black Horn could not take her back from. He hoped that place was at Ft. Supply.

They mounted and galloped off into the night.

Past midnight, he told her to rein up. The horses were breathing hard, snorting and blowing, and they settled into a walk. He felt grateful to Don Reyas that they were such strong animals.

"Did Black Horn send that Raven to find rifles or someone with them?"

"I don't know. Did Whitney and this Malloy have rifles?" she asked.

"Don't know that. I was only thinking out loud. Black Horn was determined to buy a large shipment of rifles. Do you know how he got the express box full of money?"

"I heard the squaws say that a Cheyenne in winter camp told Black Horn where his people buried it after they killed four white men. Black Horn took six of his own men and rode up there, but it was on a white man's land and they had a fight before they dug it up. His brother was killed. They scalped people all the way back for his death."

"The horses are cooled," he said. "Let's stop here and sleep a few hours. Then we'll ride into Ft. Supply."

"We're that close to the fort?"

"We should be."

"If this is our last night. . . ."

"No doubt it will be," he said, busy undoing his latigos.

"Then I want to sleep with you. Don't ask me why, but I fear tomorrow and what it will bring. I have never seen you look away because I'm soiled. I know that look in a man's eyes." She hugged her arms, and he saw her shudder. "I want to be held."

He took her in his arms. "Let me unsaddle these horses, and then we can hold each other all night."

"You won't hate me?" Tears spilled down her face.

"I only hate those who have hurt you."

Her arms tightened around him. "Oh, Slocum—"

He managed to free himself for a moment, and quickly hobbled the horses. When he rose, he glanced back to the south. What was it about those buffalo hunters that bothered him the most? That squaw man had no robes staked out. The Whitneys had some, but not many. Strange, unless Malloy had just arrived. Slocum shrugged it off. Obviously they weren't on his trail, and except for the distant howl of some wolves, he and Sugar were alone with the stars.

She stood waiting beside their unfurled bedrolls. Her long slender legs could be seen below the shirttail. She had already shed the britches that tightly hugged her shapely butt.

He toed off his boots, undid his gunbelt, and let it drop. Then he unhitched his pants and stepped out of them. She moved to him and hugged him, and their mouths met. The fiery collision touched off fireworks in his brain.

He soon cupped her shapely breast and shoved the shirt off her shoulders. Filled with a growing desire, he dropped to his knees and began to kiss her rock-hard nipples. She crushed him to them and moaned breathlessly, "Yes!"

His hand soon sought the silky skin of her inner leg, and she widened her stance for him. He traced over her moist opening with his fingertips, and she moaned louder. Then, in a flash, she was on the bedroll, pulling him on top of her. Sug's long calloused fingers gingerly sought him. She soon pumped his sword to a stiff erectness, and he plunged it inside her.

"Oh!" She gave a long wavering cry at his entry, and her muscled belly arched to meet his. They were one: lost in a tornado of volcanic proportions. Muscles to muscles, they sought destruction of this fierce need within. Faster! Harder! Deeper! Their intensity became static lightning flashing over the horizon, striking and dropping a trail of sparkling ashes that lighted the entire sky. Then, in the final moment, she began to shout, "Yes! Yes!" When everything was strained to the utmost, they both exploded, and collapsed in a spent pile.

Still connected, they fell into a dull sleep. Later, chilled by the night air, he pulled some covers over them and cuddled around her form. With her firm butt nested in his lower belly, his arm thrown over her, they slept.

In the predawn, he smoked a roll-your-own. Sitting cross-legged, he studied the soft purple eastern sky where the sun would soon crack with golden light. She lay in a fetal position, hands under her face, asleep. What would become of her? She deserved more than a crib in a brothel. How could he help her? He felt uncertain, even disappointed, at his lack of answers.

"You ready to ride?" she asked, sitting up and stretching, so her teardrop breasts pointed at the sky.

"It depends what you mean."

She hugged her arms and nestled her breasts like puppies. "You have a mean way of talking, Slocum."

He smiled at her. "All in how you take it. We better get to going. We should make Ft. Supply by evening."

"Oh," she said as if disappointed. "I planned to stay all day here with you."

"Damn sure be nice, but we better get to riding."

"Slocum?"

"Yes."

"Thanks for last night. I won't fear what Ft. Supply will offer me. I won't fear nothing ever again."

He nodded that he'd heard her as she rose and pulled on her britches. On his feet, he went for the animals. He and Sugar could chew on their dry jerky breakfast while they rode.

Under the climbing sun, he saddled their horses while she rolled up the bedrolls. Soon they were tied on, and he boosted her in the saddle. With a friendly clap from him on her tight pants, she looked down and truly smiled.

"I'd almost say I owe them damn Comanches for leading me to you."

He swung up in his own saddle, rubbed his mouth with his calloused hand, and shook his head at her as the first rays of dawn came over the far rise. "Only, you can't count on me being there."

She chewed her lower lip and nodded. "I understand. Let's ride then." With that, she booted the horse out with her bare heels.

11

"Where's this Black Horn's camp at?" Malcolm asked as they ate breakfast. The campfire smoke kept swirling around in their faces.

"Girl! Where's that chief of yours?" Vin asked plenty loud.

"Camp." She rose and pointed to the south.

"How many days from here?" Vin held up his fingers. She showed two and nodded.

"That suit you?" Vin asked Malcolm.

"Dealing with Comanches, they say, is treacherous business," the old man complained.

"Don't worry none, she's our ace in the hole. He sent her to find me to come trade with them."

"What if it's some kind of a damn trap?"

"Don't worry. I tell you, this will be the easiest money you ever earned."

"Break camp, boys," Whitney said. "We're going hunting this red devil's camp. And Malloy."

"Yeah?"

"This better be good."

"You want to be paid now?"

Whitney shook his head and stalked off. Vin turned to

look for Raven, but she was already harnessing the mule. He could get used to having her around. She screwed like a bitch mink every time they crawled in his bedroll, and she didn't have to be told to do much. What kin was Black Horn to her anyway?

"Hey," he said, looking around when he joined her at the wagon. "Is Black Horn your brother?"

"No, me him wife."

He whirled around to be absolutely certain the others hadn't heard her words, and crowded close. "Don't tell them a thing, you hear me?"

She nodded woodenly.

His wife! And him piling on her ass every night like there was no end. A knot in his stomach began to nauseate him. For a moment he thought he might puke. His wife. Oh, damn! Would she tell him? What a mess. Now he had something else to worry about.

"Does he know . . . I mean, he knows you're out here?"

She nodded and then climbed on the seat. "He sent me get guns."

"Why?"

"I speak English good and I fuck good too, huh?" She nodded and smiled smugly at him.

He looked into her brown eyes as he prepared to climb in the rig. She damn sure did both good enough. Her English was not as good as her other talents, but fair enough. Either that chief wanted those guns bad, or she wanted some new adventure. Hmm. How did she figure out Vin would get those guns? Chance maybe. He clucked to the mule and followed Whitney's larger rig.

At midday they reached the Canadian, and the boys set up camp. Vin set out on horseback to scout for the Comanche camp. Old man Whitney rode upstream, Vin down. He left her in camp with the three boys, with instructions for them to guard things and be on their toes.

From a distance, he found and studied several large Indian camps, but did not ride down close to check on them.

He wouldn't recognize Black Horn's anyway. He turned back. She'd know her own camp. He wished he had taken her along, and regretted it as he trotted his horse back upstream through the head-high willow growth in the Canadian bottoms. But in the morning he could bring her down there and be certain.

When he came up the flood plain through the willows, he could hear the shouting and laughter. He frowned. The boys must be having a party. He rose in the stirrups, but could not see anything until he rounded a grove. Then he spotted the youngest boy with his pants at his knees, his bare butt shining in the sun, poking it to the bare-assed squaw from behind as she was bent over a barrel.

Vin flew into a rage. He charged into camp slashing and whipping at the boy, who couldn't escape the onslaught with his feet entangled in his pants. The wide-eyed squaw took off running, and when the boy fell down, Vin charged his horse after her. Filled with blinding rage, he reached down and caught her by her hair. But the horse shied when she screamed, and it darted sideways. Vin fell off his horse in the process, and landed on top of her in a pile.

He soon was straddling her and slapping her face. Then, with her pinned down, he drew out his skinning knife. She needed a lesson. She knew better than to screw everyone— he planned to notch her a little with his blade. But the older boys' powerful hands drew him off her.

"We was only funning. That boy never had none in his whole life. We're sorry, but hell, man, she's just a squaw. Never figured it would hurt nothing."

"Let me up!" Vin shouted at the two older ones pinning him to the ground.

"Only way is if you forgive us and him."

"All right, I do."

The boys looked at each other and relented.

Vin rose to his feet and brushed off the sticks and grass that clung to his clothing. The squaw lay cowering on the ground, her dark eyes filled with uncertainty. He went over, jerked her up by the arm, and with her in tow, headed for his own wagon.

He couldn't let her out of his sight again. Not until the gun trade was over. A wave of revulsion went through him. She couldn't be trusted alone. And he sure needed her to find Black Horn.

For over an hour, Slocum had seen the hatless riders appear on the eastern horizon. They kept a parallel course with them. He could barely see the color of their mounts, but figured they were mostly paints and piebalds. He and Sugar definitely had company out there.

"Indians, ain't they?" she asked quietly over the calls of noisy ravens.

"Yes, a handful," he said, wondering how much farther Ft. Supply was from their location. The wagon tracks wound northward, and he felt they would eventually lead them there. One thing worried him the most. If he and Sugar ran, could they reach its sanctuary before their horses gave out?

"What will they try to do?" she asked.

"Cut us off, I figure, if they can."

"What do you plan to do?" she asked.

"Keep moving," he said. "I want to choose the place we fight them, if we have to fight. Let's lope these horses awhile."

"Slocum, I don't want them to take me alive." She looked at him with pleading eyes from under the sombrero.

"I hear you," he said, and set the gray horse into a long lope.

He looked again for the war party. They were still out there. He wondered what the change in speed would do. There were perhaps a half-dozen bucks in the party, more than enough for him to fight if they were crazy enough to attack.

The horses ran easily through the thick shin-tall brown grass. The drumming of their hooves sounded as if the earth below was hollow. They soon topped a rise, and Slocum looked off to the southeast in time to see the bucks were quirting their horses to catch up.

He shared a tough nod with Sugar, then motioned for her to go ahead. They started down into the next long sweeping swale. The fact that the braves were whipping their horses meant they would not to be denied so easily. Slocum shook his head, listening to their own horses' deep breathing and the creaking strain of saddle leather. Those bucks meant business.

There was no place to stop and defend themselves. No trees, no rocks to fort behind, nothing but a sea of brown grass. He felt uncertain what he wanted to find, and wondered if such a fortification even existed out there.

A check over his shoulder told him enough. He saw the bucks, bent over their ponies and coming on. The war party was charging up their back trail. Still a great distance behind, but pursuing them.

The horses were making it, but they couldn't lope forever. It was only a matter of time. Those bucks out there would ride their own horses into the ground. He had a higher regard for his. They'd best find a place to make a stand.

"That buffalo wallow," he said to her, and pointed to the depression. From the bowl he could survey the entire country. If those bucks wanted to try them, this might be the only defensible spot for miles.

"What will we do?" she asked.

"Stand them off if necessary."

"But . . ."

"I know, but I don't know of anyplace else out here where we'd stand a chance in a running gunfight."

She rose in the stirrups and squinted to look northward. "You don't know how far away Ft. Supply is?"

He shook his head and stepped down. He quickly hobbled the gray. She did the same to the bay. The wallow was dry, and in the center perhaps six feet deep. It had been rooted out years before by buffalo seeking to escape biting gnats and flies. Then grass had healed the scar, leaving a bowl that held water in the rainy months.

He jerked out the Winchester, listening to the gray's soft snorting.

"Get the canteens," he told her, taking the saddlebags off and wishing for a hundred rounds more than he knew they contained.

He carried the saddlebags to the south rim and spread the ammo on the ground to be ready. From his position, he could see the bucks like small sticks hurrying their horses, and catch some of their shouts on the increasing wind. Like far-off raven cries, their sounds came and went.

She threw down a bedroll to belly down on, and he nodded his approval. Raised up, she counted the attackers. He saw her lips move with each number.

"Five is all I see."

"That's plenty."

"They look like Kiowas."

"Could be," he agreed, and stretched out his brass telescope.

"A Kiowa once tried to buy me." She nested herself belly-down on the ground cloth beside him.

"Black Horn wouldn't sell you?"

"No." She shook her head and looked off at the Indians. "He wanted to have me to stuff his thing in my mouth and show off to them." She drew a deep breath. "That sumbitch did that to me every time someone came there to show how he controlled a white woman."

Slocum raised up on his elbows and studied the first rider in the scope. The upper half of his face was painted black and the lower half white. The eagle feather in his hair danced in the wind.

"Look and tell me if that is the one who wished to buy you."

She took the scope. After a moment's study she put it down. "They're Kiowas, all right. His name is Brown Bear.

He's a tough breed." She shook her head in dread. "He carries many scalps. The only breed I know that leads a band. Oh, Slocum, can we hold them off?"

"We better," he said, rolling over and sitting up. From his right boot, he drew out a small .30-caliber Colt.

"This is yours. Don't shoot it until they get close. Try to take them out with it." He handed her the pistol.

She looked at it, wet her cracked lip, then nodded at him. "They'll pay a big price first."

The Kiowas kept coming. He wondered if they knew he had chosen a good place to stand them off. Hatless, he lay on the ground, using the saddlebags for a bench rest. In his mind, he wondered about the party's commitment as he took repeated aim without shooting at the riders, who were coming nearer by the minute.

"When will you try to shoot at them?" she asked, pulling down the tail of her shirt.

"When they get in range of old Betsy here," he said, patting the fully loaded repeater in his hands.

"That'll be real close, won't it?"

"Too close. If I'd had a Sharps rifle, I might have taken one out by now." No need to have regrets. He didn't have a long-range gun. The Kiowa didn't either. Best that he could tell, they had single-shots. One carried a black-powder rifle and it might, if used properly, be the best armament of the party.

Grateful the wind swept the pestering flies away, he drew out his Colt and slipped a cartridge in the empty chamber under the hammer to have six shots in it.

"I can reload the rifle for you," she said, holding the small revolver in both hands.

He drew out a handful of cartridges. No need to spook her about the small number he had. Perhaps forty rounds. No, he made a quick check with his fingers inside the saddlebags. Less than that even.

"Good," he said. "I'll give you the rifle when I empty it."

"Slocum?"

"Yes."

"We're going to whip their damn asses, ain't we?"

"I plan to."

"Good," she said. "I know you will."

He looked again at the bucks through the glass. They were talking, and soon whipped their ponies toward the rise. He took aim at the lead rider, bent over the neck of a bald-faced chestnut pony. Quirting the animal on, he rode ahead of the others by twenty feet.

The rifle's muzzle blast thundered. The black powder smoke was quickly blown away and the Kiowa threw up his arms. His long gun went high in the air. Hit hard in the chest, he fell off the pony, which dodged to the side.

Slocum levered in a shell, drew a bead on the one closest to him. He could see the brown bare skin of the buck's back as he bent over his horse's back. Slocum aimed carefully, steadying the rifle on his elbow resting on the ground. This needed to be a good shot. With the buckthorn sight's V on the brass bead of the front sight, Slocum squeezed off the trigger.

Again the muzzle blast shattered the air. A small cloud of black gray smoke went off in the stiff breeze. The bullet found its mark, and the buck pitched forward facedown off the piebald. This time the other three bolted away to the side, with the loose riderless horse passing them in flight.

Slocum opened the lever and ran a rod down the barrel. He made quick checks of where the Kiowas disappeared, and drew the cleaning rod out.

"Don't need it fouled up," he said, and settled back down.

The three bucks were circling out of rifle range. Obviously they were busy talking about this turn of events. Slocum rubbed his whisker-bristled mouth and looked hard at them. They could quit and ride away or they could revenge their fallen brothers. Knowing Indians, he figured revenge might rank high in their thoughts at the moment. Still, he had seen them turn tail at smaller losses, to return another day when they had better odds of winning.

Indians were not the fierce soldiers Slocum had known in the Civil War, where men stood face-to-face across a field and fought until the other side wilted. An Indian fought the battles he could win and fought them where he could win them. This battle would only be a personal vendetta for the bucks.

Their yipping and screams carried to Slocum and Sugar as the three bucks sat their dancing ponies. The powwow continued. He could see the black-yellow-faced chief waving his rifle, decorated with copper tacks, at Slocum and Sugar, swearing revenge.

No matter, there were two less. With the odds so reduced, Slocum felt more confident than he had in hours. If five had overrun their position they would have lost. Three were not that awesome for him to consider. He needed to take one out at long range, the second one halfway, and the third before he penetrated their defenses. All possible, but still not a sure thing.

He dried his palm on his pants and shared a nod with Sugar, beside him on the ground. The breeze tousled her hatless short hair, and her blue eyes peered back him with a questioning look.

"They coming back?" she asked.

"They will, I figure, just for pride."

"Yeah, be the man thing, huh?" she said, and shook her head in disapproval. The wind had lifted the edges of her hair and, without her hat, made it stand up. It rose like a rooster comb. She realized, and plastered it back down with her hand. "They won't get much scalp off me."

"They ain't getting any," Slocum said, and rose to his knees at the sight of the black-yellow-faced buck riding toward them with his right hand held high.

"What's he wanting?" she asked, looking filled with suspicion.

"Guess he wants to parley."

"About what? We haven't got a damn thing to talk to him about."

"Better to talk than fight," Slocum said, and stood up.

She tackled him around the waist. "Where are you going?"

"To see what's on his mind."

"No! It's a trick. Slocum, don't go. Please, don't!"

"He's unarmed. Wants to talk."

"What good can it do?" she pleaded.

He pried her fingers from his waist. "I'll go see."

"Oh, Gawd!" she cried, and threw herself down on the blanket. "You'll be killed, I know you will—oh, don't go—please!"

Slocum strode from the wallow. The Kiowa booted his horse in to meet him. A loud-colored paint, the well-muscled animal stepped proudly through the grass, each stride showed his agility and spirit. No doubt a great buffalo-hunting horse.

"Who are?" the Kiowa demanded.

"Slo-cum—I go in peace, Brown Bear."

"How do you know my name?"

"You're a famous Kiowa chief."

"Why did you kill my braves?"

"You tell me why you follow a man."

"You have a boy with you?" Brown Bear acted like he needed a better look at her. Slocum didn't care if he did or not. He wished she had on the hat. She would be harder to tell from a boy.

"We are only passing through," Slocum said.

"Why are you here? This is Kiowa land."

"I am going north." Slocum nodded in that direction. "It was the only way to get there."

"You are a scout for the blue legs?"

"No, I am a man going his own way."

"Then go your way. You have killed two brave brothers. There will be hungry children cry for food when the winds from the north blow."

"Then their fathers should have hunted buffalo and not me."

"We will meet again, Slo-cum, and I will kill you." His eyes narrowed, and the black paint at the corners formed hard wrinkles.

"You better come early in the morning, for it will only be after the damnedest fight you've ever had." Slocum glared back at the man. *He* could look tough too.

"Death to you and all the white men who invade my land!" Brown Bear pointed his arm and flat hand at him like a sword.

"Death to you too."

Then Brown Bear turned the fancy paint stallion around on his heels and rode off to join the others. His yipping carried above the drumming of hooves. Satisfied the fight was over, Slocum turned and went back to Sugar.

Ashen-faced, streaked with tears, she rushed from the wallow to hug him.

12

The next day, Vin and Raven rode in search of Black Horn's camp. At the first one they approached, she shook her head.

"No. This one Cheyennes." When she proceeded to ride toward the tepees and cooking-fire smoke, he hesitantly followed her. His stomach curdled at the prospect of entering their camp. She was Injun and could go there safely enough—but a white man? He looked around, wishing he could hide under the floppy brim of his hat.

Several grim-faced bucks came out of their lodges and took up their weapons, rifles and bows with quivers of arrows. She spoke sharply to a squaw, who answered her, then shook her head.

"She don't know where Black Horn has moved to," she translated to Vin.

"Do the men know?" he asked, reining in his horse and keeping his eye on them.

Raven booted her horse up to one with a rifle in his folded arm and asked him. The buck shook his head and then pointed to the southeast. She nodded and rode back to where Vin sat his horse. His bowels felt ready to go off and he needed to piss badly, but filled with jittery distrust, he turned his horse and followed her from the camp. Every inch of skin underneath his shirt and vest itched. The hair on his neck rose. He expected at any moment to be shot or struck by an arrow.

"They say he is south," she said. He pushed in close beside her to hear her words, hoping the Indians in the camp wouldn't shoot one of their own.

"We can go that way," Vin managed to say to her, despite the sharp pains in his lower intestines. He dared not turn and look back or peek for fear they might reconsider and kill him. Damn, this Indian business could get real serious before he traded those rifles away.

Back at camp, he explained to the old man how he'd questioned the Cheyenne for the chief's whereabouts, and had learned that Black Horn was further south.

"You rode right in that Cheyenne camp?" young Malcolm asked, sounding impressed by the story.

"No problem. Those people ain't out to kill traders," Vin said, and pushed out his chest.

"Damn, I'd figured they'd scalped you and left your bones for the buzzards."

Vin scoffed away the boy's concern. They would believe he was a real Injun trader after this incident. It wouldn't hurt either for them to think he was a big man among the heathens. What they didn't know about him throwing up his guts after getting over the hill from the camp wouldn't hurt either.

"We better move south in the morning," he said to Old Man Whitney.

"Fine, but if this wild-goose chase goes over a week, you owe us another hundred," the old man said.

"No problem. I'll pay you that and a bonus too when we find him."

"Just so you remember," Whitney said, and spat out into the night.

Remember. He'd remember the old goat. They had the best deal they could make out there, and were still demanding more money. He might leave the whole bunch of Whitneys for the buzzards when he finished making his transaction with Black Horn. He still hadn't forgiven them for letting that boy screw his squaw. It might have been all a big game to them, but it sure had made him mad as a hornet.

He decided to turn in. They needed to get up and move on come daylight. Besides, he needed a little squaw tail before he shut his eyes. He never did get enough of her. He told them good night and went to his quilts.

After undressing, he shook her bare shoulder to awaken her, then lifted the covers to let himself under them. He dropped to his knees and jacked on his shaft. She raised her legs and grinned in the starlight at him. He scooted up close and nosed it in her. Then he dropped down and began to pile-drive her.

She grunted and humped away until he finally came. Exhausted and satisfied, he lay on his back and studied the thousand stars.

"Best damn thing I ever did was find you," he said, patting her on the hip. Then he rolled over and went to sleep.

Vin dreamed about the war. He recalled being on patrol and finding a haggard old woman dressed in rags hiding in a root cellar. Her gray hair was all stringy and her brown eyes were so wide they looked like saucers when he jabbed his bayonet at her. It had been months since he had been with any woman. Maybe if he . . .

"Take off your clothes," he ordered after deciding any flesh at all, even old stuff, was better than none.

"Huh?"

"You stupid? I said, take off your damn clothes. Now be quick about it!"

"What're—ya going to do to me?" She fumbled with the buttons on the dress front in the shadowy light that filtered down the stairs into the cellar.

"What do you think?" he said, setting the gun aside and undoing his belt. The sour mildewed smell of the cellar went up his nose as he looked apprehensively at her dried-up breasts and the wrinkles of loose skin across her shrunken belly.

"Get down on the floor on your back. You know what I want."

"Oh, don't do that to me," she began to moan, but she obeyed him.

He forced down his pants, and the damp ground felt cold on his knees when he fixed himself between her legs. Grateful it was dark, because she was ugly and reminded him of a witch he once knew back home, he pushed his half-hard erection in her. She gave a cry and turned her face away.

Wild shooting and shouting began outside. He jumped to his feet and jerked up his pants. Be his luck to get shot by some Confederate skirmisher. Damn, if they had only waited a few minutes more. His rifle barrel out in front of him, he started up the stone steps out of the cellar. His eyes blinded by the bright light, he spotted a Reb in butternut clothing rounding the barn.

Vin took aim, shot, and missed. But the man stopped and returned fire with a pistol. One bullet smacked into the cellar's open trapdoor. Close enough. Vin retreated into the cellar backwards.

He could hear the old woman moaning at the foot of the steps, and some crows calling off in the distance. The skirmisher soon disappeared, and the rest of Vin's company arrived. The old woman was captured and interrogated by the scouts. Of course, he knew what they did to her. It was three agonizing months later before he found another available woman. Then it was some old fat whore lying in a crib who charged him two dollars, and her snatch proved to be as big as a washtub.

He woke up with a start, thinking he was in bed with that fat one. Shaking in the night's cold air, he reached for Raven, but she was gone. He threw back the cover and peered into the night. He could only make out his mule and horse. Her pony wasn't with them. He slapped his forehead and fell back down. Oh, shit!

13

Slocum on the gray, Sugar on the bay, they rode up the street of tent saloons and stores. No one was in sight except a fat dove in a sheer gown who stood in the doorway of one tent marked "Privates' Club." The fat around her waist pressed hard at the pink material. Her small breasts were partially exposed, and she forced a smile at Slocum and Sugar.

"You boys horny?" she asked.

"Not that horny," Sug said.

Slocum snickered, and they rode on under an abusive barrage of the whore's cuss words.

He stopped at the tent marked "Gilbert's Mercantile," and dismounted. "We might find some food to cook in here."

Sug agreed, and swung her leg over the saddle, dropping heavily to the ground. They hitched their horses and went inside.

"Howdy, folks. What can I do for you?" the gray-haired man wearing an apron asked.

"I want a box of .44-40 ammo, for one thing."

"Ain't got much ammunition. Oh, I've got a few boxes left. Expecting some guns and ammunition any day. Arney

Freight's a-bringing me a large shipment of arms and ammo from St. Louis."

"Wait—you said Arney Freight?" Slocum looked the man in the eye.

"Yes, why?"

"Might been a coincidence, but I saw a tarp with their name on a wagon that was down on the Canadian."

"Was he lost?"

"Hell, I'm not certain. How many rifles were you expecting?"

"Forty."

Slocum looked at Sug, and both said the words at the same time. "Black Horn's rifles!"

"What do you mean Black Horn?" the man asked. "He's a Comanche, ain't he?" He blinked, obviously realizing for the first time that Sug was a woman.

"Right, and he's looking to buy some rifles."

"I ain't selling him any."

"We know that, but your rifles and ammo may have fallen into some greedy hands."

"I could sell several of those guns if I had them right now," the man lamented.

"Yes," Slocum agreed, and pounded his fist on the counter. "After we get some food, we better go see the camp commander about this. He needs to know about Malloy and the rifles."

"Captain Slade?"

"He the commander?"

"He's gone right now in the field. There's a new lieutenant from back East is out there. Good luck."

"First, we need some food. You have any meat?"

"I can carve you some buffalo meat. Got a fresh-killed fat cow carcass hanging out back."

Slocum looked at Sugar, and she nodded. "Go with him," he said, and the man showed her the way to the rear of the tent. While they were gone to get the meat, Slocum went to the open front flap and studied the street. A familiar figure in buckskin with his arm in a sling rode up on a jaded roan horse.

The fat whore gave the buckskinner an inviting smile, but he shook his head and pushed the roan on. He narrowed his pale blue eyes and looked hard at Slocum.

"Well, bless me soul, if it ain't old blood and guts himself!" The buckskin-clad man drew a leg over the horn and slid to the ground. "Man, it is you, ain't it, Slocum?"

"Sam Durant, never before seen you turn down anything that walked, crawled, or ate grass."

Durant cast a quick look over his shoulder at the big dove, and then turned back and laughed. "I have got a little fussier in my old age. What the hell are you doing here?"

"Trying to keep my hair."

"Hell's fire, this is the worst place in the world for that."

"What happened to your shoulder?" Slocum asked, looking hard at the sling.

"Took me a bullet in the armpit. Crazy story, but I'd buy a jug of whiskey and tell you the whole thing."

"Can't, but get some whiskey and we'll cook up the meat she's back there getting right now."

"She's getting?" Durant acted taken aback. He spat a wad of tobacco out on the dry ground and wiped his mouth on the back of his hand. "You ain't told me—" Then he swept off his great brown hat and smiled at Sug standing in the doorway.

"Sam Durant, meet Sugar Irons."

"My extreme pleasure, ma'am." Durant made a bow at the waist. "However, I must apologize for my friend here, who hides all the beautiful women in the world that he can find from me."

"Pretty bad at that, is he?" she asked.

"Oh, yes, ma'am, he is a scoundrel of the highest resort. While I, my good lady, am a gentleman of means and property."

Slocum shook his head in amusement. "That means he owns this roan horse and the buckskins he's wearing."

"Wrong, my friend. I have purchased the Delgotto land grant."

"What in the hell is that?" About to laugh out loud, Slocum frowned at the man's words.

"Three thousand acres of mountain stream and pastures in New Mexico."

"Hell, I am impressed. I better pay the store owner. Don't run off with this Don Durant," he said to her, heading for the counter.

"You think that man you saw has my rifles?" the store owner asked.

"It explains a lot about why he was down there."

"Those rifles—"

"What rifles?" Durant asked, coming through the door and obviously interested.

"Arney Freight is supposed to be bringing me forty Winchesters and ammunition," said the store owner.

"No, they shipped them to you several days ago in the care of one Vin Malloy," Durant said.

Slocum blinked in disbelief at the man's words and shared a frown with Sug. How did Durant know about the shipment? And if the rifles ever reached Black Horn, the entire countryside would be afire.

"How do you know about this Malloy?" Slocum asked.

"I got him to thank for this shoulder. Lots of funny things been going on up there at Dodge and they all point to Malloy. First someone slick-like the other night stole four or five repeaters from scabbards on horses tied at hitch racks. They couldn't find who took them or what they did with them. Then, out on the prairie, some sodbuster's wife was murdered, raped, and scalped. Oh, they tried to make it look like Indians did it, but the only thing gone was a Winchester. Indians would have taken a lot more than that." Durant flexed his wounded shoulder and made a sour face. "An old drunk hunter told me this Malloy was trying to buy repeaters. Paid him a big price for his old Spencer and wanted to know where he could buy more."

"Then," Durant said with a sigh, "I met this Arney and learned he hired Malloy to deliver rifles and ammo down here. So I saddled up and rode to see if he had delivered them. Malloy's got him a Comanche squaw. That's what caused this." He motioned to his shoulder. "Me and him had an altercation over her in an alley."

"She's one of Black Horn's wives," Slocum said.

"We know a whole lot more now, don't we?" Durant said. "Storekeeper, you have a couple good bottles of whiskey?"

"Sure do. Some golden rye."

"Get us a couple of bottles. Me and this old hoss here have a million lies to tell each other. He claims this fine lady is the best damn cook in the Western Hemisphere, and we are going to socialize a little this evening while she fixes our supper."

Durant waved away Slocum's offer to pay, and paid for the liquor himself. Slocum dug out the money for the coffee, beans, rice, flour, meat, and other items Sugar had stacked on the counter. They left the tent store with three tow sacks of food.

"Good place to camp up the stream here," Durant said with a nod in that direction as they mounted up. They took his lead while he lavished his conversation on Sugar.

"Tell us about your hacienda," Slocum said, breaking into his wild stories about bygone days.

"Oh, it is lovely. All it needs is a hostess like you." Durant twisted in the saddle and nodded toward Sug.

Slocum noticed her face redden under the tan. She looked away, uncomfortable, and tried to ignore his brazen suggestion.

"Sug is a Texan," Slocum said.

"That's what I like about her is her Southern elegance. It shines through and amazes me."

"Durant, she can outrope and outshoot you." Slocum grasped his saddle horn in both hands and shook his head in disbelief at the man's line. Durant sounded more serious about her than he could imagine.

"That wouldn't be all wrong," Durant said, and turned to her. "You don't have a husband, do you?"

"No, but I am recently divorced." she said softly.

"That's good."

"You aren't interested in who was my ex-husband?" she asked him with a frown.

"Hell, no. But who was he?"

"Chief Black Horn of the Comanches."

Slocum listed to the cawing of the crows over the wind. A red-winged blackbird clung to a breeze-swept willow, and some plovers on thin legs ran ahead of them. Above the soft hoofbeats of their animals and the roan's deep snorts, they rode a ways in silence.

"Aw, hell, girl, it don't matter one bit to me who you was married to," Durant said at last. "I'd of divorced that stinking sumbitch too. Place to camp's right up there."

They all laughed.

14

The next morning, Vin wished for eyes in the back of his head, so he could see everywhere. Raven was gone. She hadn't come back either. He took his food with the Whitneys.

"Where's she gone?" the old man asked, sounding suspicious.

"Went to see Black Horn." Vin didn't look up from studying his coffee. "She'll be back. We need to head south and find his camp."

"Why she up and leave?" Malcolm asked, taking a seat beside him.

"Injun women go hide when they have their monthly thing," Vin said. "Bad luck to be around a man when that bleeding starts." He looked up to see what effect his lie had on them, and the Whitney men agreed. Of course the youngest boy only shrugged, as if he didn't know what Vin was referring to. The two older sons and the father understood about such things, and that was all that mattered; he had her sudden disappearance explained satisfactorily.

Where and why had she run off? They must be close to the Comanche camp. Had she told him everything that those Cheyennes told her? Maybe she knew where her husband was and had gone there. Vin felt grateful he had the four Whitneys to back him. It might take all their guns to hold off the heathens if they knew he had so many fine rifles. He couldn't get over the strongbox full of money that she had mentioned. It brought cold chills to his arms under his shirt despite the sun's warmth.

The only thing he had to count on was her talking to Black Horn and telling about the trade for the rifles she had promised Vin. The Comanches couldn't get that swap anywhere else. Besides, he'd risked a lot simply coming out there.

They broke camp, and Grant drove Vin's wagon for him. That left Vin free to ride Clunny and go look for signs of the camp. He trotted the horse to the rise, and all he could see were more waves of brown grass. How far away could the camp be? He soon thought he had found tracks of her barefoot pony, and took off in a southwest direction. If he could follow her prints, he could find Black Horn. Every few feet, he swiveled around in the saddle to look for signs and to be certain there weren't Indians sneaking up on him.

His mouth was dry as cotton. He wished for some whiskey. He strained to see the horizon, but nothing but heat waves materialized. He pushed the horse harder. Her tracks, if they were her tracks, had vanished into the thick mat of dead and green grass spears.

His horse snorted, and woke him from his trance. What was he doing out there? This gun-trading business had become worse than buffalo hunting. He'd had the boy Sid to help him skin and make some company for a while. But one night, the kid had choked on some buffalo meat that got caught in his throat. He'd turned blue, gasping and holding his neck. There'd been nothing Vin could do for him. Sid had simply died. After that Vin had hated being out there—all alone.

He'd gotten to hearing things. They'd sounded like Indians on a raid, or women crying for help on the wind. So when at last he went into Ft. Dodge to sell his stinking hides, he'd had the stone ache so bad it made him sick to his stomach. Then he'd found Raven, or maybe she'd found him. Damn mink bitch anyway.

Why did she run off? He hadn't beaten her since the incident with the boy. Injun women didn't mind beatings. They got them all the time from their husbands. Lots worse ones than what he gave her.

He checked the sun time. Be time to rest and let the animals graze soon. Maybe he should go back to the wagons. Nothing out there he could find. Where was Black Horn anyway? Would she come back? He had no idea.

The second day, they swung east. The old man was growing more upset with each passing mile, and Vin figured he would need to pay them something or they'd quit on him. Grant drove his mule, and Vin took off to search. The old man rode the country south, while Vin rode ahead, topping the rises and looking.

"No sign?" Vin asked the old man later when he dropped from the saddle. It had been another fruitless day for him. He'd found some old weathered lodge poles and a long-dead horse. But nothing else.

"Nothing but a few buffalo."

"I didn't see them," Vin said, and wiped his gritty forehead on his sleeve. He stunk like a horse. Many more days like this and they'd be out of everything but his guns.

"We need to talk," Whitney said, and Vin's heart quit as the three boys closed in around him. What did they want? What were they up to?

"We know that you aren't trading them red niggers no beads and blankets," the old man said, folding his hands over his chest. "You've got new rifles under that damn tarp. We looked and found them today."

"Well," Vin said, thinking of a way to weasel out on these dumb hicks. "Injuns ain't interested in beads and blankets. They've got plenty of them."

"Plenty, huh?"

"Sure. Why, traders been out here giving them that wampum deal for years."

"How many hides you figuring to get for them rifles?" Whitney asked.

"Plenty," he said, suppressing a sigh of relief.

"That's why you need us and our wagon?" Grant asked.

"Sure," Vin said. "No way I could haul them all back without you. Hey, I'll give you a bonus too."

"Ain't there something illegal about trading them guns?"

"Ha, it's illegal to make whiskey without stamps too, but folks do it."

The old man nodded. "We don't give a gawdamn about no stamps or making whiskey. From here on we're your partners, not no gawdamn hired hands. We split this hide deal fifty-fifty."

"But I paid for them rifles," Vin protested.

"Figure that up," the old man said.

"I figure they cost me over a thousand bucks."

"How much them Injuns going to pay you?"

"I'm going to ask for twenty hides per rifle," Vin said, hoping to mess them all up with arithmetic.

"Lord, that's a hundred dollars apiece at Dodge!" Malcolm said.

"That boy, he's had lots of schooling," Whitney said.

"That's right," Vin said, not certain himself of the amount.

"Then there should be three thousand to split after your expenses of one thousand," Whitney said, doing some figuring with his fingers. "Half of that is fifteen hundred dollars or three hundred hides."

"Sound fair enough?" Malcolm asked.

Vin surrendered, not knowing what else he could do. He gave the old man a Masonic handshake, and Whitney nodded to him. "These boys are going to join the order when we find one out here."

"Good," Vin said, and shook their hands. "Partners," he

said, and wished he knew where the bitch was at. He looked across the prairie, but saw nothing. Not even a cloud. The perennial wind roared in his ears, and he wondered how far away Black Horn's camp might be.

15

"How in hell's name did you end up with a three-thousand-acre land grant?" Slocum asked. The fire's small flame shone on Durant's beard in tones of red and orange. He sat cross-legged across from Slocum. They'd managed to drag in enough wood for a cozy fire, and Sug busied herself doing dishes while the two men passed the bottle and reminisced about old times.

"Found me a mother lode. I was up in Colorado, high-country hunting and killing time. I'd shot an elk, and had it hanging high in a tree and wrapped in canvas, so the damn magpies couldn't peck holes in it. Went down to the creek to wash my hands and face. Too cold to take a bath up there."

Slocum rolled a cigarette and lighted it. He offered the makings to Durant, but the man shook his head.

"There in that water was the biggest nuggets I ever had seen. They looked like melted candy that had hardened up again. I thought it was fool's gold and picked a piece up. Then it struck me the damn thing was a gold rock big as a hen egg. It scared me. I'd seen color before, but this one was real. It was huge."

"Well, was there more?"

Durant nodded, and by the glint in his eyes, Slocum deduced his story was true.

"I worked that gravel for five days. Weather got even colder. I shivered all the time. Found a lot more. But I soon had it all in that area. I mean, I had the fever so bad, I was shaking from both being cold and about to piss in my pants at the realization I was richer than a St. Louis banker.

"Then the damn Utes found my camp. I seen them sneak in the valley. Hell, I'd left my rifle, saddle, horse, tent, the meat. They took it all after not finding me. I laid low for twenty-four hours. Then I decided I better hit the trail since I was riding shank's mare to get back.

"I stashed most of the gold, took a good-sized sack, though, and a rag of a blanket the Utes had left me. Took me weeks to find my way out and avoid them. They got real close a couple of times. I finally came out at Walsenburg."

Slocum tried a deep drink of whiskey from the neck of the bottle. It was hot going down, but it settled him. Then Sugar came to join them and listen to the tale. She passed the bottle back to Durant, who tried a snort and wiped his mouth on the back of his hand with a big "ah."

"I hired me some tough men and rode back," Durant said. He took out a plug of tobacco and sliced off a chunk to place on his tongue.

"Them Utes didn't give up easy. We had a running gunfight for two days on the Rio Grande. Took potshots at each other. Had a couple Sharps rifles, though, so we won that. I made a run up there, got my stashed gold on a mule, and came out a-flying to join them boys.

"We had to fight our way back out, and I kinda figured we'd get someone killed, but only had two fellas even get wounded, and they were only scratches. But them Utes fought hard."

"How much was all that gold worth?" Slocum asked, taking a deep drag on his cigarette.

"Thirty thousand dollars."

"Whew!"

"I have pissed off fur catches, blowed away good pay, spent money on whiskey, and—pardon me, ma'am, but good times with ladies. This time I said, 'You old coot, you better buy something tangible that will last you the rest of your life.' "

"So you bought the hacienda?"

"I did. Got sheep and cattle and folks to take care of it for me."

"What the hell are you doing at Camp Supply then?"

"Looking for that no-good sumbitch who shot me in Ft. Dodge. I was headed for St Louis, and stopped over to spend the night, and, well, you know the rest."

Slocum shook his head. "You'd make a wonderful liar. Who else could find that much gold washing his face in a creek?"

"It's the honest-to-Gawd truth."

"What were you going to do in St Louis?"

"Look for a woman to share this hacienda with."

Slocum looked at the stars for help.

"Darling," Durant said to Sugar, "You heard my story. Now what do you think?"

"I won't promise you a thing, Sam Durant. And you could decide better too. I mean, you may not want a ex-wife of a Comanche, and I ain't exactly a sit-in-the-parlor lady for some big rancher. And besides, I may not want you. That being truthful enough?"

"Whew, yes." He wiped his forehead of imaginary sweat.

"Good," she said, and pitched some grass stems on the flames. "Oh, and another thing. I came here with *him*." She indicated Slocum with a thumb. "I ain't quitting him till he quits me."

"By damn, a woman knows what she wants. You're like my granny. She never minced no damn words. Loved that woman." Durant took another swig, offered it to her, and she passed it on to Slocum.

"Now, what are you going to do about this Malloy and them guns?" Slocum asked.

"I'd like to nail his damn hide to the—excuse me, ma'am—shit-house door."

"Don't go excusing yourself around me," she said. "Say what you think, 'cause I damn sure will do the same."

Durant grinned like a big fat cat with a pile of fish before him. "I like that, Sugar."

"Let's go talk to the army in the morning," Slocum suggested.

"Good idea."

"You two can sit up and drink whiskey all night," she said, standing up and jerking the blanket she'd sat on over her shoulder. "I'm going to find some sleep."

"Thanks, Mother," Slocum said after her. "Glad we have your permission."

She turned and looked at them both mildly. "Guess a girl could do worse. Having two men in her camp."

"A lot worse, Sugar, darling," Durant said, and winked at her.

Slocum raised the half-empty bottle and studied the level through the glass. Orange and red from the firelight glinted off the liquor. He put the bottle to his mouth and took a deep swig. Somewhere out there, this Malloy had rifles for Black Horn.

He considered the matter, then shook his head. Let the damn army capture Malloy. Besides, it was no skin off his butt if that belligerent Comanche got those guns. He couldn't go around the world righting every wrong.

"You think that gal's serious about going back with me?" Durant said, still looking off into the darkness where she had vanished.

Taken aback for a moment by the man's question, Slocum nodded slowly. "I think she might be. She's been through lots of hell. Told me that there was no way for her to go home to Texas. Her paw and brothers would never accept the fact she'd been an Indian's squaw."

Durant nodded, leaned over, and took the bottle from Slocum. "Folks got strange ways about them. I know what she means, but hell's bells, you can't live in the past. You and I have done things better left undone. We damn sure wouldn't make the same mistake again, but they ain't letting us be. You still on the run?"

"Yes."

"Hell, I thought that was over years ago." He shook his head in disgust, raised the bottle, and took a deep draught of it. "Whew, good whiskey. They ain't down here looking for you, are they?"

"Not yet." Slocum cracked a smile at the man's seriousness. "Hell, Durant, they have to have work."

"Well, I'm damn grateful they're not after me."

"Gets to be part of you after a while."

"Looking over your shoulder?"

"Looking ahead and sideways too."

"I really figured that would be over by now. Man, that is bad. You ain't sore about me taking a shine to her, are you?"

"No. I was concerned about her, in case I had to take off."

Durant handed the bottle back. "Don't worry. If she and I don't dance, I'll be sure she gets a square deal out of it."

"Fair enough." Slocum took another swig. The whiskey settled him and he felt peaceful. His belly was full of rich buffalo meat she had browned on the fire, and fluffy rice along with skillet corn bread. A man could do a whole lot worse.

He listened to the mournful cries of some wolves. He'd been out there like them before too, with his belly eating up his backbone, penniless, and riding a spent horse.

He recalled being somewhere near the Verdigris River in the Indian Nation. It had been sleeting lightly since sundown. A party was going on at a cabin on the flat below him. He stayed in the timber for cover while coming downhill. The whine of a fiddle carried across the frozen landscape, and the familiar tune of "Turkey in the Straw" made his stomach churn. Sounds of laughter and happy voices resounded from the lighted house, and rang out into the cold night. Pecks of the sleet tapped on his canvas coat; he carefully approached the homestead.

Their joyful voices rang out with shouts as the dancing inside continued. There were several wagons and rigs parked around the place to indicate it was a large gathering. Slocum moved behind the corral and in the starlight, he looked over the array of animals. They shuffled about, shying away some when he climbed over the pole rails. He soon chose a stout bay gelding from the lot, slipped his rope over the bay's neck, and led him to the back. Slocum slipped the bars out, and soon had the horse clear.

Carefully, he examined the animal for any faults. He used his hands to feel for shin splints or any swelling of the joints and hocks. At the sound of a woman's loud laughter, he stopped and looked toward the house, but when no one appeared to be coming, he went back to work. Unshod, the horse's feet looked sound enough in the dim light. No fistula or saddle sores, and the gelding acted full of spirit. He would do.

Quickly Slocum undid the latigos and changed his saddle to the bay. Then he took his last ten dollars, wrapped it in a kerchief, and tied it on the mane of the spent horse he'd ridden in on. Be poor pay for the trade, but it was all he had. The fiddler inside the cabin struck up "Sally Good'n," and Slocum's heart about stopped. How many times had he heard that song and danced to it?

Alert for anything, he slipped the spent horse into the corral. Its head low, the animal snorted wearily at the ground, blowing flecks of the white powder aside. Then it dropped to his front knees in preparation to rolling on his back in gratitude.

Slocum eased the bridle on the bay's head, checked the cinch, and heard voices. He paused and located the two coming in his direction. Swiftly he led the horse behind the log shed. Out of sight, he listened, hoping the bay didn't stomp too much and invite their attention.

"Can I kiss you, Shirley May?"

"I reckon so, Sidney."

"You know, come spring, I'll be asking your paw for your hand."

"That's why I'm a-letting you kiss me, Sidney Brown."

Then came the sounds of their clothes rustling.

"We best get back before Paw misses me," she said, sounding concerned.

"Yes, ma'am. But I can't hardly wait," the boy said with a waver of excitement caught in his voice.

"Neither can I. Neither can I."

Then came the crush of their fleeting feet on the ground. Slocum waited. The sleet had begun again. At this rate, it should cover his tracks. He swung up on the tall bay, reined him around, and rode back into the timber. The horse picked his way up the steep hillside and through the dark trees. Slocum felt better with the fresh horse between his legs. He paused on the ridge, and while the lights from the cabin were only a small yellow dot, he could still hear the music.

It was Christmas Eve.

"What plans you got next?" Durant now asked, breaking into his memories.

"See what the army is going to do about this gunrunner."

"Then what?"

"I may try to find a man who hired me to protect him."

"Who's he?"

"A Comanchero."

"A friend?"

"Friend enough."

"Slocum, I ever need backing, I sure hope you're around." Durant struggled with the effort to get to his feet. Apparently, Slocum decided, that wound was hurting him more than he let on. For a long moment, Durant looked off in the darkness in the direction Sugar had gone. Then he turned and went the other way to bed down.

Slocum sat and stared into the fire for a while. He watched the flames lick up in red and blue to consume the logs. Then the wolf pack howled again, going over the far rise. He knew their ways too.

16

Vin Malloy felt beside himself. No sign of the squaw or the damn Comanches. He pushed Clunny to the top of the rise, and blinked his eyes when he looked over. There were riders coming. Hatless ones. Was she bringing Black Horn to trade with him? Or were they other Injuns? Damn, he wished he could see better. At last, he hoped, he was going to get the trading done and get the hell out of there. But what if it wasn't her band?

A chill of fear ran up his spine. No, that was Raven riding beside the bare-chested one on the piebald stallion. He better get back to camp and tell the Whitneys. He turned Clunny around and started back for camp. How would he ever get the Whitneys to believe that he was getting buffalo hides for those rifles instead of money? Didn't make any difference. He'd kill them if he had to.

All he needed was for them to back him while he traded. Once he had that money, he could ride out of this godforsaken sea of damn grass. It all looked alike, and there was nothing out there but damn birds that squawled and ran about on the ground on stick legs. It would be good to get back where there were real trees and white people.

He short-loped the sorrel for camp. The Comanches were

coming. He repeated it to himself over and over. His heart
ran a thousand beats a minute, and threatened to jump out
of his throat. He could not believe his good fortune. At last,
he was going to trade with her husband. He hoped the man
wasn't jealous.

Hell, he'd bet all that redskin wanted were those guns.

"Boys! Boys! Where's the old man?" he asked, jumping
off his horse.

"Out there," Grant said, pointing. "What's wrong?"

"The Comanches are coming to trade."

"Wow. Hear that, boys?"

"Yeah. How many of them are there?"

"Maybe fifteen. I never counted them too close."

"Malcolm can," Collie added, getting up. "He can count
all the flies on a dead bird."

"He counted to a thousand once," Grant added, standing
on his toes to get a better look.

"Be good to get this over with," Vin said out loud. "Oh,
they're coming. They'll find us, all right." He went to get
something to eat from Malcolm's stew pot.

"That's Paw coming like his pants are on fire," Collie
said, rushing over to get his rifle.

Vin could see the old man whipping the hell out of his
horse. His plug hat and flapping coattails made him look
like something from another world. What the hell had his
bowels in such an uproar?

"Buffaloes, boys! There must a thousand head over
there!" he shouted, out of breath and pale-faced.

"A thousand head?" Malcolm asked with pained disbelief
written on his face.

"Yeah, I never seen so damn many of the woolly bastards. Why, there's a fortune just to the west."

"Comanches are coming to trade," Vin said, disturbed
that their greed for hides might coax the Whitneys away
when he needed them the most to back him.

"You sure?" Whitney cut his dark eyes around to glare
at Vin.

"I seen them. They're over the rise to the south. Be here in an hour."

"You sure they'll give ten hides a rifle?" the old man demanded with his questioning eyes black as coal.

"They don't, they ain't getting them. Why, any of these red niggers out here will give that for one."

"All right, but if they don't and we miss that many buffalo hides, I'll stomp your ass in the grass." Whitney's eyelids slitted to lines in his anger.

"You'll see. You'll see."

"I damn sure better, or me and the boys are quitting this wild-goose chasing and getting us some robes to sell."

Vin went off to eat his stew. He kept glancing at the ridge, wondering what was taking the damn Comanches so long to get there. They couldn't be that far behind him.

"They know that we're here?" Grant finally asked, cradling his Sharps in his arms.

"Comanche, like all Indians, know more than a white man does about where folks are at."

"What if they rode past us?"

"They're coming." He looked down at his half-eaten bowl of stew in disgust. Those bastards were coming, pure and simple.

"Looks to me that if they were pissants they ought to be here by now."

Vin spotted the rider on top of the far ridge. He stood up and grinned with newfound confidence. "Here they come now."

"Who is it?"

"It's Raven," he said, and wondered in the same instant where the rest of the warriors were.

"Thought she had the whole party coming with her."

"She did. Maybe they're laying back to see if we're ready to trade," he said, feeling more confused by the minute about why that bare-chested chief on the piebald wasn't right on her horse's butt. He watched her race the bay mustang toward them.

She drew up the pony short of the four expectant men. She narrowed her brown eyes to the sun's glare, and fought with her horse to make it stand still.

"Where's Black Horn?" Vin asked, stepping up to stand beside her horse.

"Him come few days. Found plenty buffalo, go hunt first." She gave a nod to the west.

"Shit!" Vin swore, and threw his hat on the ground.

"Maybe they needed more hides to trade with us," Malcolm said, then looked at his brothers for approval. They agreed.

"He gawdamned better come," the old man threatened.

The squaw, unmoved by their upset, slipped off her horse and started to lead him toward Vin's wagon. For a minute Vin was taken aback. She'd returned, and obviously was ready to be his until the chief came in from the hunt. Aw, hell, he wanted this gun-trading business all over.

Slocum looked at the private carrying the rifle on his shoulder. The early morning sun shone on his blue uniform. Slocum dismounted heavily. He shoved his hand in his pockets to get the pants down, then handed the reins to Sug.

"Private, is the lieutenant in this morning?" Slocum asked the guard.

"No, but Sergeant Kelly is, sir."

"Ask the good sergeant to come out and talk with us. We have some information about the hostiles."

"Yes, sir. Your name?"

"Slocum, that's Durant, and she's Iron."

The young man blinked at her in disbelief, and then his face grew red with embarrassment.

"Hell, ain't you ever seen a woman before?" Durant asked in impatient disgust, and dismounted.

"Yes—" The private swallowed hard and rushed to the wall-sided tent that served as headquarters.

"Damn, why, they must raise them boys in confinement anymore," Durant said, cutting of a slice from his tobacco plug and deftly feeding himself off the blade. He winked at Sugar, and she smiled back at him.

Kelly soon appeared, a six-and-a-half-foot-tall beanpole with a handlebar mustache white as snow and green eyes that could bore holes in dried oak.

"Gentlemen and lady." He doffed his field cap to her. "What news do you bring?"

"There's a man out there with fifty or so repeaters fixing to trade them to a Comanche called Black Horn."

"And what be this rascal's name?"

"Vin Malloy, best I know," Durant said, moving into the conversation.

"Your name, sir?"

"He's Slocum, I'm Durant."

"How do you know all this?" the noncom asked apprehensively.

"First the bastard tried to kill me. Then I found out he had the rifles that were supposed to be delivered to a merchant here, but he went on to sell them to Black Horn."

The noncom knit his salt-and-pepper brows into one. "How far away is he?"

"Couple days south by now." Durant looked to Slocum, and he agreed with the estimate.

"My commander is in the field with most of the troops," said the sergeant. "I could hardly spare a half-dozen men to go and search for this gunrunner."

"Hell, we just came by to tell you," Durant said in obvious growing disgust.

"I appreciate it. But you can see the riding animals I have left are all rejects." The man indicated the broken-down mounts in the nearby corrals. Several coughed with symptoms of chronic colic. Raw saddle sores could be seen on their withers even at a distance. Several hobbled or limped when they tried to mill around. Slocum considered the lot of them as less than good crow-bait. In fact, shooting them might put them out of their misery.

"Slocum, we've wasted our damn time coming over

here." Durant gave him a wry look of disapproval, turned, and took his reins from Sugar.

"Oh," Durant said, prepared to mount up. "You tell that damn General Sherman we told you about this slick and his guns. So when he gets the casualty list that these guns caused, he can stew over it too." He swung into the saddle and checked his horse. "Come on, we've got better things to do than talk to a blank wall."

"Where is the lieutenant in charge?" Slocum asked the tall noncom before he mounted his gray.

"In the guardhouse for his own security, sir. According to the surgeon, the poor lieutenant has become deranged."

"That mean he went crazy?" Durant asked, pushing his horse in closer.

"Yeah," Slocum said, and swung in the saddle. "Military will do that to you. Especially out here."

They rode out of the small base camp. Hammers were ringing as roof rafters were being framed. Several new sod-walled buildings were being built by civilian workers, no doubt to serve as warehouses. Slocum knew this camp's name came from its being a quartermaster depot to put the military's needs closer to the hostiles than Ft. Dodge, where the supplies came in on the Santa Fe Trail.

"What are we going to do next?" Durant asked.

"I sure hate to see Black Horn get those Winchesters," said Slocum.

"If he doesn't have them already," Sugar added.

Both men looked at her and grimly agreed.

"What do you want to do, Sugar?" Durant asked.

"I'd say go try and stop him from getting them, if there's a chance he don't already have them."

"You might be risking capture again." Slocum frowned at her hard.

"No." She shook her head. "He won't take me alive."

"Sounds like we need some supplies and a pack animal for this adventure," Durant said.

"That's what they call this place, Camp Supply," Slocum

said, and shared a nod with the two of them. The big if—if they were in time to stop the trade. He shook his head to dismiss his concern for Sugar's safety if she went along. He would like to leave her at the outpost. She'd never consent to that. He booted his horse to keep up with them.

The black mule they traded for to pack their supplies was called Jules. He was a tail-wringer that someone had recently trimmed with shears. He acted full of spirit while they loaded the panniers hung on the cross-buck saddle with food and items that they would need for their extended stay on the Llano Estacado.

"You fellas going buffalo hunting?" the young clerk asked, bringing out an armload of items.

"Yeah," Durant said, bent over busy resetting a shoe on his roan horse. Sug never said a thing, and Slocum nodded, taking the items from the clerk. Slocum wanted to laugh. Poor boy had no idea that under the broad-brimmed hat and doing the actual packing was a female. It was hard to tell with her dressed like a boy, and she wasn't talking much.

It was midday by the time they had their horses' shoes checked and were ready to head south. Slocum wiped his sweaty face on his shirtsleeve and handed Sugar the lead to Jules. The temperature had warmed up considerably and the wind had died down that day.

He checked his cinch and mounted the gray. The gelding danced some until he reined him in. They left with a nod, and the young clerk waved after them like a boy left on the wharf when the sailing ship was leaving port.

On the dim road south, they met their first wagons of returning hunters. A tall lean man rode out in front of the three rigs, with several hunters and skinners on shaggy-maned ponies. Their leader raised his hand to stop the train, and with his Sharps balanced across his lap, he spat tobacco off to the side.

"Howdy," Slocum offered. "You boys get enough hides?"

The mustached man shook his head. "No, but we've damn sure had enough Injun hell. Ain't worth it. They're sure stirred up. Killed one of the men day before yesterday, and wounded two more. Like a nest of hornets, they're stinging and ain't no letup. Besides, we never found the main herd. Only stragglers. Ain't worth it." The man spat again, wiping his mouth on the back of a long suntanned hand. "I'd sure warn you, it's been tough and there's damn near a dozen of us."

"Appreciate your concern. You haven't seen a two-wagon outfit? Whitney's his name, got some boys and a squaw man calls himself Vin Malloy?"

"Nope, but there's lot's of outfits still down there. They're just a lot crazier than I am. I can find something else to do besides lose my life to them heathens."

"Obliged," Slocum said, and Durant agreed.

"I'd swear that was a girl," the man said with a grin at his discovery of Sugar.

"You can swear, all right," Slocum said, and booted his horse on. "She is one."

"Well, I'll be twitched." He removed his dirt-floured wide-brim brown hat and gave her a nod. "Nice to see you, ma'am."

"Thanks," she said with a charitable smile. Then she jerked Jules's lead and rode past him.

They met two more outfits that afternoon. Both were tired of the Indians' hostile actions and were headed out. Neither had seen Malloy's bunch.

The sun formed a red ball on the western horizon when they finally made camp. His face windburned and hot, Slocum was anxious for the night's coolness to set in. He was worried that they'd had no word on Malloy's whereabouts. The man could be anywhere in this sea of grass. Worse yet, the guns might already be in Black Horn's hands.

"We should reach the Canadian by tomorrow night if we push hard," Slocum said, taking off the first pannier. He struggled under the weight, but soon set it on the ground.

Durant joined him to help, and they removed the second one together.

"How far you reckon they've gone?" Sugar asked, on her knees, busy making a chip fire.

"No telling. Black Horn has to keep moving to feed his horse herd. So he's no doubt been traveling too. Plus he needs to kill some buffalo to feed his band and also dry some meat for winter."

"He could be anywhere down here," Durant added, and Slocum agreed. *Anywhere.*

With the horses unsaddled and hobbled at last, Slocum finished putting rope hobbles on the mule and turned him loose. He straightened and with his hands on his hips, flexed his stiff back muscles. Where was Don Reyas? Had he completed his trading and headed back for New Mexico? The man's situation concerned Slocum as he studied the last orange and purple light of sunset.

17

Enraged, Vin stood with his hands on his hips and fought for his short breath. If that worthless Black Horn was so damn interested in getting those rifles, he'd better get over here. He could chase them damn buffalo anytime after they made the trade.

Raven grinned at him, then quickly dismounted her pony. "You miss me?"

"Hell, yes," he said, looking around. The Whitneys looked off the other direction, as if searching for the buffalo and the Indians. He didn't care. He considered her filthy deerskin dress and what it contained. It had been a while since he'd had any. Then, wondering how long the Indians would take to hunt, he glanced off in the direction of the unseen buffaloes for a final look at nothing but the grassy horizon, and shook his head in defeat. He turned on his heel and glared at his rig, still mad about at the Comanches' delaying actions.

"Guess we wait?" Malcolm called after him.

"Yeah, all we can do. I'll be back," Vin said, taking Raven by the hand, anxious to make some distance between him and the others for his own reasons—her body.

"Don't do nothing I won't do," Grant said after him.

"I won't," Vin said, herding her and the pony along toward his wagon.

She acted as if it suited her, and even grinned at him once or twice before they went around the far side of the tarped-down load. It offered some privacy. He didn't care who saw him screw her, but being too brazen might give those horny boys the idea that they needed a little too. He was in no mood to share anything with them.

He motioned to the bedroll, and she quickly began to shuck her deerskin skirt. Then, bare-assed, she dropped to her butt and took off her moccasins. She obviously wanted him to see her slit, for she turned it toward him with her legs apart. He leered down at the triangle of pubic hair as she slipped the last shoe off. Then he toed off his boots, thinking about what it would feel like to be in her again. His fingers trembled with anticipation as he undid his galluses and dropped his pants. The wind swept the skin on his bare butt.

He dropped to his knees and waited for her to wrestle off the blouse over her head, exposing her small tits. By this time, the fiery need to have her consumed him, and he followed her down, moving between the legs that she raised so he could stuff his dick into her.

With a cry of pleasure, she raised her butt as he pumped in her to force it in deeper. She threw back her head and screamed out loud. He looked around, peeved at her outburst; no need for those boys to know he was having this much fun. Harder and harder he drove. She pulled him down on top of her. Gurgling and gasping, she strained, then issued a deep sigh.

He looked down at her and frowned. Hell, she must have come. Her glazed eyes soon opened and looked up at him. She had a small smile on her copper lips. She soon resumed her action underneath him, and he began to become enthused too. With a new fervor, his butt began to drive it to her. Her mouth soon was open, and drool ran from the corners as she tossed her head and strained. Her small breasts with their rock-hard nipples bored two holes in his chest. Then he felt the thrilling realization that he was about to come. The anticipated pleasure quickly clouded his mind and sent him skiing down a snowy slope. He thrust himself to the very bottom of her mine, and exploded with a depleting force that wrung every ounce of energy from him.

He rolled off her and lay on his back, closing his eyes to the bright sunshine. Spent, he blinked in disbelief at the three boys standing over him.

"We come to share this Indian pussy with you," Grant announced.

"You—" Vin sat upright, but noted that Collie, the quiet one, had slung Vin's gunbelt over his shoulder.

"Yeah," Grant said. "We're having us some of this Injun pussy. Don't worry none, little girl. We just going to have some fun."

Vin watched the oldest of the brothers push down his suspenders and drop his pants. His dusty pink half-erection looked to be of horse-sized proportions. The large-framed boy scooted forward on his knees, talking to the girl, who looked a little wide-eyed and afraid at this new situation.

Resigned to the inevitable, Vin nodded for her to go ahead. Then he turned his back on them, rose, and pulled on his pants. He could hear Grant's shout when he scored contact with her. Damn, he needed them too badly to back him at the trade for him to start a big fight over her. Besides, what would a few more dicks mean to her anyway? She'd probably like it.

Vin went back to camp, and poured some leftover coffee in his cup. He squatted down on his boot heels and studied the brown horizon. How long before those bucks had killed enough buffalo?

"Figured you'd get sore about them horny boys of mine screwing her," the old man asked.

"Why?" Vin asked, as mildly as he could.

"Well, lots of men take women like her as private property sometimes."

Vin looked down at the dark bitter-tasting coffee in his metal cup. It was as bitter as the fact that he'd let them have her, but the task for him now was convincing Whitney he really didn't care. Far more important was the gun trade and their presence. If laying her kept them there, why should he give a damn what they did to that brown bitch?

No matter how hard they tried, they'd damn sure never wear her out. Then Vin wanted to laugh at his thoughts. No, they'd not use it up. With disdain at the boys' noisy shouts coming from beyond his wagon, he squinted at the bright rolling brown land. He hated this godforsaken tree-less country, hated the damn fears that roiled in his guts over the upcoming trading with this red bastard. If only he had it over with and was headed for St. Louis with a wash-tub full of money. Over the sharp smell of the swirling campfire smoke, he imagined he could smell lavender per-fume again. The same kind that those fancy fat whores used in St. Louis. He wanted to inhale lots of that.

Then the notion came to him. When it was all over, he'd have to kill all four of the Whitneys. It would be him or them. He might share some skinny little brown whore with them, but he damn sure had other ideas about the money from the rifles. That was his. No shares, no deals. He wanted all of it.

There they went again. Yelling at Malcolm for him to give her more of his dick. That kid wouldn't be long at it. What was this, his second time? Vin drank some more of the bitter coffee. Better figure out a good plan how to kill all of them when the trading was over.

18

"Don't look east. We've got company," Slocum said under his breath to the two of them as they rode.

"Who and how many?" Durant asked, his hand rested on the butt of his pistol.

"I've seen two bucks so far on the left. They've been spying on us the last few minutes. One or the other would come up on that rise, then quick get out of sight, but they must be paralleling our route."

"Comanche, Cheyenne, or Kiowa?" Durant asked.

"Looks Cheyenne. I seen an eagle feather in one's braid."

"How many do you think there are?" Sugar asked. Her blue eyes looked straight ahead.

"No telling. Probably a hunting party of young bucks ready to fetch some scalps and horses to take home and brag about. I would guess they're young, or we'd've only seen one of them before they'd attacked, if we'd've seen even him."

Durant agreed. "Where you want to try and den up?"

"We should make the Canadian by dark. Bent's adobe corral down there is the only thing besides a buffalo wallow we can find to hold them off."

"That's still several miles?" Durant asked with a frown.

"Yes. If we find anything else on the way, we'll use it. Them bucks might get tired and go home too."

"We have that repeater of yours, my Sharps, and some pistols is all," Durant said as if weighing the effectiveness of their armaments.

"You can pick off the far ones. I can hold down the charges," Slocum said with a grin. Lord only knows how well those bucks liked eating lead. Most didn't, and left in the face of strong opposition. "Let's lope."

"Yes," Sug said with a dark look to the east. "They say Cheyenne are worse than Comanches."

"No," Slocum said to reassure her. "You've been with the worst."

They used their heels to push their mounts into a gallop. Slocum cracked Jules hard on the butt with his reins, and sent the tail-wringer loping after her. He took one look back, saw nothing, but the hair on his neck stood up at the prospect of what he knew was behind them. Bloodthirsty renegades. He recalled the head buffalo hunter's words as he licked his sun-dried cracked lips. *They were all mad as hornets.* He urged the gray on.

By late afternoon, their lathered mounts breathing hard from the push, Durant pointed to a mesa on their left. The hill rose sharply on all sides, and then flattened on top from what Slocum could see. No way that a war party could scale it without coming under sharp fire from the defenders.

Slocum glanced back. No sign of them, but he felt they were coming as sure as sundown would come in a few hours. No water up there. The three had little more than what their canteens held. If the Indians kept them pinned down up there for a while, it was taking a big chance. But the sweaty hard-breathing horses would soon be done in at this speed.

"Try it," he said, and Durant swung to the side. They reached the base and drew up. Then Durant took the lead at Slocum's wave, and Sugar nodded, jerking the reluctant mule after her.

Slocum reined up, dismounted, and took the brass telescope from the saddlebags and studied the country to the north. He saw them. With care, he counted seven riders on lathered horses. Good, they would be too tired to scale the mesa on horseback. He looked up the steep slope as Durant and Sugar moved to the side to climb up. There would be no head-on charge up that sharp a slope. That too would slow down any attackers.

He collapsed the scope and remounted the gray. This could be a good choice or his death site—one or the other. There would be no second chance, as hard as those bucks were coming. They wanted blood and scalps.

The horses were hobbled in the center of the acre of the tabletop. They snorted in repose. Durant went to the north rim and looked for the war party. Slocum went to scout the other sides to see if there was an easier way up. The south side looked too steep to consider. If the Indians came at them, he decided it would be the northeast corner, where the mesa joined a row of hills and there would be half as much slope for them to gain.

"They'll come from there." He pointed it out to Durant, who was using his telescope to search for them.

"More than likely. I haven't seen them in a while. They may have other plans."

"If their ponies are half as tired as our animals, plus being grass-fed, they might not be in shape to charge us."

"You have a point. What about her?" Durant asked with a nod back toward Sugar. "She's tough as cast iron. When she had a chance to get out of this damn country, she stayed."

Slocum looked back, and saw she was busy building a small fire. Sug Irons was tough.

"She ain't no tea-party woman," Slocum said, and took the scope from him.

"Gawd, no, but she's something else," Durant said, sounding impressed.

"They're coming. They must have figured on our plans. They're riding that long hogback and coming this way."

"I better get my Sharps."

"How much ammo you got?"

"Thirty rounds, maybe more." Durant paused and glanced at Slocum with a questioning look.

"It could be a long siege," said Slocum.

"Yeah, I'll make them count."

Slocum nodded, and went back to scoping the warriors through the glass. Must be a dozen, they looked young. Most bucks were young. They didn't live long. With buffalo hunting, war parties, and white man's diseases, it was hard to live past thirty. Kind of their way. Life held little for them when they were old and unable to participate in the things that their male society held dear—courage and the ability to take coup on an enemy.

"How many are there?" Sugar asked.

Slocum turned and looked into her blue eyes. "A dozen. Young ones out proving their worth."

"Many guns?"

"Half have rifles, the rest have bows, it looks like."

"I'm not afraid," she said, sticking her chin out in defiance. The fresh south wind swept her short hair up in a rooster's comb.

"I figured that you weren't worried."

Her blue eyes drew to slits, and she looked hard at the far-off figures coming toward them. "Oh, I'm worried. I still have nightmares of Black Horn, but the two of you have given me strength."

"Durant's serious about you," he said under his breath. He could see that the man was busy loading his rifle by the horses.

"I know. In time, I'll consider him."

"Guess we have to get by these bucks first."

She nodded. "Yes, and we will." Then she went back to

the campfire. Slocum turned back to watch the Cheyenne.

They grew close enough that their war cries sounded like distant ravens on the wind. Durant came over, lay down on his belly, and used a small cross-arm to support the long rifle's barrel. He tossed a few blades of grass up, and with care set the windage on the back sight.

Slocum hurried after his own rifle. How would the bucks come at them? Suicidally? No telling. He hoped the action of Durant's long gun would shut them down. If they came hard enough, the bucks would overrun them.

"You better come be close," he said to Sugar.

She agreed with a nod and rose from her fire. They both hurried across the mesa to drop to the grass beside Durant. Lying on the ground with her between them, Slocum could see there was no holding the Indians back. The war party never hesitated at the base of the mesa. Their lathered ponies, grasping at their bits and jaw straps, charged the hillside.

"Hold your ears," Durant said, and rose up to take aim.

The rifle's loud report sounded, and a buck in the lead threw his hands up, hit hard in the chest. The shot spooked the others, and they went to the side. Durant ejected the cartridge and jammed another home. He lay back down to take aim and fired again.

The second buck went off his pony in a cartwheel that meant he had been hard hit. By this time, the Cheyenne boys were taking notice, and several had pulled in their mounts as if to reconsider this attack. One, on a black piebald, let out a hair-raising scream and charged straight for the mesa top.

The Sharps roared, but not as loud, and Durant swore aloud. "A damn dud!" He fought the breech open and jammed another round in place.

Slocum rose to his knees as the horse and rider bore down on them. The buck was lying flat on the horse's back, making any shot hard. Slocum squeezed off the first round, and sent the pony into a facedown spill that dislodged the rider.

Undeterred by the fall, the painted-faced buck jumped to his feet and came on. The rage in his throat reverberated over the ridges and echoed back. Slocum's lever-action rifle barked again and then again. Both bullets slapped into the Cheyenne's quill vest. The first one cut off his screams, and the second one tossed him backward down the hill.

Durant's Sharps roared again and again. The Cheyenne soon had had enough and left the field. Sug used the scope, and at last said, "There are only five left."

"Five too many," Durant growled, and brought his cheek hard against the rifle stock. The Sharps belched again, and the next Indian was sent headfirst off his horse. The others, obviously shaken by the distance of the shot, quirted their ponies and rushed away to a more secure place further north on the long hogback.

Durant rose to his knees. The wind whipped his buckskin fringe as he nodded. "Damn, it takes a lot to change their minds."

"Thanks," Sugar said, and beamed at him.

"We better not act too confident. I say we ride to the Canadian and try to stop this gun trade," Slocum said, getting to his feet and brushing off the loose dry grass.

Durant wiped the corners of his mouth with the side of his thumb, and then with a twinkle, nodded to her. "Damn, he's bossy."

"Guess he's the boss," she said with a shrug.

"Guess so. Whew, old Sharps here sure saved the day," Durant said, using it for a brace to get on his feet.

"They sure ain't stopping out there," she said, and pointed to fleeing specks.

"Sugar," Durant said, draping his good arm over her shoulder. "I'd sure like for this wild-goose chase to get over. It is a damn sight more peaceful at my ranch in New Mexico, I promise you."

Slocum saw her nod at his friend and let his arm rest on

her shoulder as they came back together. He shoved the Winchester in the scabbard and then went around and drew up his cinch latigos. Those two might make it yet.

Where in hell was this Malloy and those rifles?

19

Filled with frustration and about to burst over the damn
Comanche Black Horn leaving him sitting there while he
hunted, Vin looked across the grass sea for a sight of them.

"You tell him I had his guns?" he asked Raven, squatted
by the small cooking fire.

She didn't answer him, and didn't move quick enough
to escape the toe of his boot. He reached out and snatched
her up by a handful of hair.

"You tell him about the rifles?" he demanded in her face.

Her brown eyes wide with shock, she managed to nod
her head.

He released her. Dumb girl anyway. No wonder Black
Horn had sent her as bait to lure him out there on these
godforsaken plains. If the chief wanted their damn guns so
bad, what was he doing out there chasing damn buffalo?
He could always do that. Maybe the Cheyennes wanted the
guns. But he didn't recall seeing a mountain of hides
around their camp.

No, he was forced to sit and let those Whitney boys
diddle her whenever they wanted to—to keep them from
running off and leaving him out there alone. The whole
thing was a mess. Only her word about a trunk full of

money had made him stay this long under the glaring sun.

Why didn't Black Horn come on in?

"We've been thinking we might go kill a few buffalo while we're out here," Old Man Whitney said, coming over to speak to him.

"Better not. It might piss some of them other Injuns off and we'd have to fight our way out of here."

"I don't like sitting out here." The old man rubbed his neck and shook his head. "Makes me itchy."

"Make everyone itchy, but by damn, he'll soon come and we'll trade him them rifles and get the hell out of here."

"How did you make this deal anyway?"

Vin shook his head. None of his damn business how he did it. "I made it, all right. You'll like your share of it."

"I'm getting nervous—just sitting here."

"I'll do something if he don't come by sundown."

"Yeah, you better." Whitney turned on his heels and went back to where the boys lounged around the wagon.

Raven brought Vin a tin plate of half-cooked beans and fatback. He sat down cross-legged on the ground and motioned for her to bring him some coffee to wash it down with. The hard nuggets of beans tasted bitter when he chewed them. She wasn't much of a cook either. Black Horn must have sent her because she was the worst cook he had.

She squatted on the ground a few feet away from him, waiting for his next order. It was strange to him that she'd come back. He'd figured that once she'd gotten back to her people, he wouldn't ever see her again. A quick glance at the sky, and he figured it must be midmorning. By sundown he needed to do something about Black Horn. Old Man Whitney was going to be hard to stall much more.

She jumped to her feet and used the side of her hand to shade her eyes.

He looked up. Someone or something was coming. It didn't look like armed warriors on horseback. More like someone leading a horse.

She said something in Comanche, then began to jump up and down.

"Who in the hell is it?" he asked, and stood up, holding his half-finished plate. With his eyes half-slitted against the glare, he could make out a woman leading a bald-faced horse.

"Sister."

"Gawd Almighty, what's she coming here for?"

The girl didn't answer him. She rushed away to greet her sister. Vin was undecided about whether to sit down and eat the undone beans or throw them away. Instead he scrapped them back into the pot. More cooking wouldn't hurt them.

"Who's she?" Grant asked, coming over.

"Her sister."

"Many more come by, we'll have one apiece." Grant laughed and made a lurid grin. "Reckon she can buck like her sister?"

"Damned if I know."

Grant hitched up his dirt-stained pants. "I'd sure try her and find out."

"Better find out who she is first. She might have a tough buck of a husband who'd use a big knife on you."

"Yeah," Grant agreed.

The two women hugged and made quite a fuss. Then Raven pointed toward the camp and took the woman's horse's lead rope to bring her in.

Vin could see this one was dressed in buckskin with beads sown on the blouse. The long fringe swept in the wind, and she even had braids. She was no Comanche squaw.

"She Blue Song," Raven said to him, and Vin nodded, admiring how her breasts pushed out the doeskin—not flabby triangles like her sister.

"She ain't Comanche?"

"No, Cheyenne."

"Where's her husband?" He didn't want to admit it, but her looks made his scrotum crawl.

"Killed by pony soldiers."

"Where's she going?"

Raven shook her head, then motioned to the kettle of beans.

"Sure, feed her," he said, realizing the Whitneys had slipped in closer for a better look. It made him angry. If anyone was going to test this squaw in bed, it was him.

"What's her name?" Grant asked.

"Blue Song."

Raven served her a plate of beans. When she tasted the first bite, she spat it out on the ground and made a face of disapproval. Vin almost laughed out loud. Blue Song quickly dropped to her knees and began to stoke the chip fire. Both women exchanged some words.

"Maybe you got yourself a new cook?" Grant said with a grin. "I'll screw her for you when she ain't cooking for you." The others joined in his raucous laughter.

The humor at his expense made the skin on Vin's face draw tight. He would enjoy killing them when the gun trade was over. Do it slowly, maybe stake them down on an anthill. He'd pour sorghum on their balls to start with, so they didn't forget their messing around with his squaws. He was the one who'd brought the guns out there, who did all the work.

This new squaw would sure enough be a bedful. He wanted her all for himself. Somehow, he had to keep their dicks out of her. She would be his when he took that trunk of coins and went west. Maybe San Francisco. Hell, it didn't matter. He would live the good life someplace. And use her until he got there.

"You aiming to share her too?" Grant asked, using his hand to work on the obvious discomfort in the crotch of his pants.

"Not right now."

"Don't be too long about deciding," Grant warned. "I could sure use her right now."

Damn, he might have to shoot him, too. The wind swept his face as he watched the three boys trail back to their own wagon. He couldn't hold them off from her for very long.

20

"That's a big herd of buffalo," Durant said as the three of them bellied down on the high windswept ridge.

As far as Slocum could see, the familiar dark brown outlines of all sizes of bison dotted the prairie. Thousands of the animals grazed spread out. This had to be the main southern herd that men spoke of. In the great basin east of the Big Horn Mountains along the Bozeman Trail, he'd seen plenty of the woolly ones. But this sight had him in awe. No way to count or even estimate the numbers out there.

"Had all those hides in Dodge, a man would never need to work again," Durant said, more to Sugar than to him.

"I'd damn sure hate to flesh all of their hides for you," she said.

"Girl, we ain't going to be doing that kind of work on my ranch. Not ever again."

"I like the way he talks better all the time," she said to Slocum with a long grass stem in her mouth to chew on.

"Hold him to that," Slocum said, using his glass to scope the countryside for any sign of Indians.

"I will," she said, and combed back her short hair. "I'll sure be glad when this hair of mine grows out again."

"You don't look bad now," Durant said.

"I'll look better then," she said, and replaced her hat, drawing up the chin string.

"See anything?" Durant asked.

Slocum shook his head at him. "Nothing, but they can't be far away."

"By this time, that damn Malloy may have traded him those rifles."

Sugar frowned at Durant as he rose to his feet. "That shoulder wound hurting you?" she asked.

"It ain't bad." He acted like he wanted her to forget his wound.

"Take that shirt off. *We* better look at it."

He tried to refuse her, but she insisted. One look at the filthy bandage and she scowled. "This needs to be cleaned and replaced. How far away is some water?"

"Canadian can't be far south of here," Slocum offered.

"Good, we're going there and clean up this wound."

"I'll be fine," said Durant.

"Maybe," she said, and shook her head. "A doctor dress that?"

"He said he was one."

"He wasn't much of one."

"Well, he did me right after he floated a mule's back molars, if that counted," Durant teased her.

"It ain't funny," she said sternly. "It needs to be redressed."

"Well, damn, guess I better obey her," Durant said as they walked back to their horses and mule.

"You better if you want to go on telling those tales," she said, and set her blue eyes hard on the animals ahead as if she had other things on her mind.

Slocum wondered as he followed them, collapsing the brass telescope, if Durant's wound was showing signs of infection. There was no way for them to amputate a shoulder. He hadn't even noticed how Durant carried that side, but the man did use his left hand a lot for a right-handed man. Obviously she had noticed the difference; maybe it was because she was paying more attention to him than before. Where were the rifles? If Black Horn had them already—then Slocum's mission was for nothing.

They reached the rise above the Canadian in midafternoon. There was no sign of any Indian camps where they dropped off the slope into the bottoms. A few straggly cottonwoods marked the course, and they were soon beside the stream. The signs of previous fire rings scarred the short grass. Wind rattled the cottonwood leaves and swept through the willow thickets around them.

"Get that shirt off," Sugar ordered, dismounting from her horse.

Slocum gathered the reins of their animals. He planned to picket them close by. The traffic of Indians in the river bottoms was notorious, and he had no plans to let a large band stumble on them.

"I'm going to mosey around," he said, and left Sugar to tend to Durant's wounds. They both nodded as she unwrapped the filthy-looking bandage.

Slocum swung aboard his horse, leaving the others hitched. He rode in close to the two of them and leaned over.

"How does it look, Doc?" he asked.

"Not very great," she said, on her knees behind her patient.

"What you going to do?" Slocum asked.

"Clean it, then maybe use some gunpowder on it." She made a pained face. "May need to burn out the infection."

"I want to scout a little. I'll be back. You behave, Sam. You need looking after."

"Hey, can't you just clean it out?" Durant said, arguing with her.

"It needs lots of that," she said, and gave him a shove to turn around.

Slocum grinned to himself at her words. Like it or not,

Durant was about to be doctored upon. Slocum booted the gray out of the clearing. Several miles downstream, riding through the near-head-high willows, he reined up the horse.

He could hear shouts and yells. Twisting in the saddle, he glanced back, saw nothing but the wind-stressed willows. With care, he dismounted and left the gray hitched. On foot, he moved carefully through the twisting brush, listening closely for the shouts and yells.

Low on the ground and searching for the source of the sounds, he removed his hat and dropped down on hands and knees to try to see the revelers. Several bare brown butts scrambled around in the clearing ahead. They climbed out of the water, their sleek copper skin glistening in the sun, while others ran and jumped into the shallow Canadian with high splashes. Perhaps a half-dozen Indian girls in their early teens enjoyed the water sport. From fat ones with large bellies to sleek future beauties with budding breasts, they acted very uninhibited, and were unaware of his presence.

They had to be Cheyennes, he decided after seeing enough of their youthful activities. They also must have a strong camp nearby for them to risk such frolicking. He decided it would be best for him to get back to Durant and Sugar. As he suspected, the Canadian River bottoms hosted many Indian camps.

Back at camp, he found Durant sprawled out on his stomach atop a bedroll. His white skin glowed in the sunlight. Slocum dismounted, and saw Sugar kneeling down beside a small fire. She was obviously boiling some rags, and drew them out with a stick.

"These are hot, they'll burn you," she warned, and placed them on Durant's shoulder as best she could with her stick. Then, gingerly, she lifted the tails of the steaming cloth until they were piled on his shoulder over the wound.

"Whew," he said with discomfort. "You're going to cook me alive."

Slocum shared a grim look with her.

"He's got an infection," she said. "It will only get worse unless we do something about it."

"We'll take him back to Ft. Supply," Slocum said.

"What about the rifles?" Durant asked.

"I can handle that somehow," said Slocum.

"Are you crazy, man?" Durant demanded from his belly-down position. "No way you can stop them."

"I don't need you half dead on me either."

Durant shook his head and buried it in the bedroll, obviously with some disgust over Slocum's plans.

"I want to burn it out," Sugar said. "It is the only chance he has. Then I agree we need to take him back. It is more serious than he lets on."

"Do what the hell you're going to do," Durant said.

"We will," she snapped. "I'll need some gunpowder."

"I'll bust open some cartridges," Slocum said. Durant would sure be unable to ride with him after that treatment. He'd need to be taken back. Even as tough as Sam was, between the infection and burning gunpowder, he'd sure be a sick boy.

Slocum went over to sit cross-legged on a blanket. He used an empty cartridge casing to loosen the lead from the first shell. After he had opened six, he poured the black powder from each one on a small piece of oilcloth she'd given him. His job completed, he looked up and met her blue eyes.

"I hope this works," she said softly.

"Me too." Slocum rose to his feet.

"He's burning up with fever."

He nodded. "We going in from the back?"

"It looks worse back here," she said as they knelt beside Durant.

"This ain't no small deal," Slocum said to Durant. "We'll have to sit and hold down both your arms."

"I figured the hurting had only begun," Durant said, lying facedown on the blanket.

"You need to bite down on something so you don't swallow your tongue," she said, looking about, then running to the horses and getting some patching leather from his saddlebags.

"You may wish you'd rode on to St. Louis after this," she warned, putting the leather strap between his teeth and lowering his head down again.

"No, I'd of missed you," he muttered with his mouth full.

The wound did look inflamed when she lifted the wet rags away. The exit hole was there too. It oozed blood on his heat-reddened skin. Slocum helped her direct the black granules onto the wound. She went quickly to the fire and returned with a blackened stick.

"This will hurt," she warned, and began poking the gunpowder into the wound.

Using both hands, Slocum piled the rest of the powder where she worked. He could hear Durant grunting with pain as she forced more into the opening.

At last she threw the stick away and moved across him to settle on his right arm and put both her hands on his shoulder to hold him down.

"Light it," she said.

Slocum readied himself to restrain their patient. He drew out a torpedo-headed parlor match from his shirt pocket. He could think of lots to tell Durant, but they wouldn't comfort the man.

"Hang on, pard," he said, then struck the match and touched off the powder.

A brilliant flare, and the smoke was blinding as he wrestled with the tormented man's arm and body. The stench of burning flesh wafted up Slocum's nose as he strained with all of his might to hold Durant down. Waves of pain must have coursed through Durant, for his entire body jolted and almost threw both of them off, then subsided, and did it again. Durant made animal sounds, biting down on the leather, and then went limp. He passed out.

Nearly blinded with sweat, Slocum's gaze met her blue eyes.

"Jesus," she said under her breath.

He agreed.

21

Vin spent all afternoon wondering how to keep the Whitney boys out of his new squaw's pussy. His belly growled all day, and churned with him thinking about screwing her. He sure wanted to get some of her tail when the sun went down. But sundown would bring the old man over demanding he do something about the rifles.

How would he handle him? Vin needed to ride out there and find out when the hell Black Horn was coming in to trade for the rifles.

Then he saw them. *Caritas*—two-wheel Red River carts, a whole passel of them coming in a train.

"What the hell they doing out here?" Grant asked, coming over.

"Damned if I know," Vin said, knowing the boy only came over to get a better look at the Cheyenne woman, who was busy sewing beads on a new blouse.

The squeak of the dry axles sounded like so many squealing pigs to him.

"Comancheros," the old man said, joining them. "Wonder what them Mexican bastards are doing out here."

"Trading with them, I guess," Vin said.

"I came out here with Sterling Price and the Missouri

Guard in the Messikin War. We whipped them greasers without a damn fight. I was just a boy then, but I hated them greasy bastards then, and still do."

"Just act natural," Vin said. "There's too many of them for us to start a fight with them."

The old man agreed with a nod. Vin could see the one in charge was out in front, leading the train, riding a big fancy horse too. Vin rubbed the grit from the corner of his whisker-bristled mouth with his thumb. After this rifle trade was over, he planned to have him a horse like that to ride.

"Good afternoon," the man in the fancy clothing said when he rode up.

"Good afternoon," Vin said, striding out to meet him. Did these bastards intend to sell Black Horn rifles too? Maybe they also knew the chief had the money. Vin would need to know if they were in competition. Damn, the man must have thirty hands or more. He'd come prepared.

"My name is Don Reyas." The man swept his wide-brimmed sombrero off.

"Mine's Malloy, that's Whitney and his boys."

"Buffalo hunting?"

"We aim to do some," Malloy said.

"Best be careful. The Indians are short on temper these days."

"You've been trading, I see," Vin said, motioning to the carts loaded with furs.

"Yes, we are going to head north soon. We are about out of goods to trade." The small Mexican smiled.

"Guess you get a big price for trading guns with these heathens?" Vin asked, to probe into their reasons for being out there.

"No, Señor, no guns."

"I mean, who would know, huh?"

"My grandfather and my father traded with the Iteha. We have never traded guns to them."

"Missing some money, ain't ya?"

"If you wish to trade guns with them, fine, but be sure they don't point them at you, my friend."

"Ha, ha. We ain't got any guns to trade them. Just figured that all you Messikins traded them anything that made big money."

"No guns," Reyas said, and started to remount. "Be very careful. They have objected to the white hunters wherever we stopped to trade."

"Let them red fuckers object," Vin said, filled with rage. Those damn shaggy beasts didn't belong to them either. He looked over at Whitney, cradling his rifle. He could see the disgust written on the old man's face for this Messikin. Then Whitney nodded in agreement to his words.

Reyas touched his hat and signaled for the train to move on. Then he remounted, obviously not going to say another thing to them. The rich bastard had come by to swagger a little at them was all. Vin would show them greasers how to swagger when he got a hold of Black Horn's money box.

Vin walked back to camp. He'd send her out to find that red pecker and get him to come and trade with them. That way she'd be gone and he'd bed that good-looking sister. Sending Raven out there might make the old man settle down some too. It would kill two birds with one rock. Ha, there wasn't a rock around this gawdforsaken place.

"You," he said to Raven. She looked up at him with a bland expression.

"You go get your mustang. I want you to ride over there and tell that Black Horn to get over here and trade with me if he wants them rifles. Now!"

She bolted to her feet, and Blue Song started to get up with her.

"No, you stay here," he said sharply to her. She settled back down and resumed her beadwork. Good, his plan was working. He'd soon have word to Black Horn to get his butt back there, and it would give Vin a chance to screw this new one while Raven was gone. Now, if he could keep

Old Man Whitney hooked a little while longer . . .

Bareback, Raven rode off on the brown mustang headed west. Vin wandered back to see if this Blue Song spoke English. He noticed the youngest Whitney, Malcolm, saddle his black horse and with a rifle across his lap, ride out at a short lope. Where the hell was that little peckerwood going? Never mind that kid. Vin settled down beside the Cheyenne woman, who was intent on her beadwork.

"You speak English?" he asked.

Blue Song nodded.

"Your man die long ago?"

"Two moons."

"Long enough for you to forget him?"

She shook her head.

"I'll help you," he said. "You can be my squaw."

She shook her head, not looking up.

His hand shot out and clamped on her chin so he could glare into her eyes. "Listen, bitch, you're mine to do whatever I wish. You savvy that?"

Her eyes drew into slits and her mouth formed in a straight line. His eyes widened in disbelief. He never had seen such an insolent squaw in his whole life. He let her go and staggered to his feet. In a flash he had his belt undone, and began to pelt her with the wide leather strap. She threw her arms up and fell to the ground. He would show her who was the damn boss. These Indian sluts needed some teaching from time to time. Those bucks didn't put up with that kind of disobedience—he wouldn't either. He lashed at her harder.

The quicker she learned her place, the better it would be. She'd learn he was a tough taskmaster and took none of her guff. At last he paused, and bent over to catch his breath, the belt wrapped in his fist. He looked down at the huddled squaw in disgust. Had she learned her lesson yet? She'd better have, or he'd beat her harder.

"Fix some supper," he said, and kicked her in the hip.

She slithered away from him on the ground, rubbing the

mark of his boot toe as she warily glared at him.

He looked off across the heat-wave-distorted grassland.

"That dumb brother of ours has run off with the other one," Grant said, breaking into his thoughts. Vin blinked at the boy in disbelief.

"Naw, I sent her to see Black Horn," Vin said.

"Read this note Malcolm left."

Vin took the paper, figuring Grant was only talking crazy. He blinked at the words written in neat penmanship on the paper.

Dear Paw

    Me and Raven are going away. We will not be back. We are going to Texas. She knows some good places where no one will find us. Do not follow cause only Indians can go there. Sorry, but I love her so much.

Your son Malcolm

"What's the old man think?" Vin couldn't see him, but he could make out the swirling smoke from their campfire.

"Figures that he went away with her," Grant said.

"I doubt it," Vin said. In truth, his guts crawled. How would he ever manage to find Black Horn and trade the guns without her? Be just like that dumb boy to be so in love with her—his first piece of ass that he ever had. Oh, hell, what had Vin done to deserve this mess?

22

"You coming around?" Slocum asked on his hands and knees, close to Durant's ear.

"You got any whiskey?" Durant managed in a weak voice.

"Very little. She's soaked those new bandages with it."

"What a waste," he said with a groan.

Slocum helped him sit up. Shocked by the man's weakness, he propped him up and held the short whiskey bottle to his lips. Durant managed to use his left arm enough to guzzle some down.

"Whew, this is tough."

"It'll soon be dark. But I want us to get out of the river bottoms. You think you can ride and not fall out of the saddle?"

"You seen anything?" Durant managed before having a coughing fit.

"No, but I'm concerned about the unrest in my guts over us staying here much longer. These bottoms are crawling with Indians."

Durant nodded and finished off the whiskey. He let out a great sigh and tossed the bottle aside. "Good stuff."

Sugar returned with some water in a canvas bucket. She

frowned at Slocum. "He ain't exactly ready to get in a ass-kicking contest."

"How's the infection?"

"I think we may have helped it. The cure was a little tough. He still needs a doctor's attention." She shook her head in disapproval.

"Closest one would be back at Ft. Supply," Slocum said.

"Damnit, I'll be fine. A couple of hours, I'll be ready to ride," Durant complained.

"Don't talk so damn brave," she said, and began to make some fresh coffee.

"One day's rest and we'll take him back," Slocum said. "I better do some scouting and make certain some party doesn't happen on us here."

She agreed with a nod. Slocum could hear the two of them bickering when he went for the gray horse. Saddled and ready, he swung up and set out for the ridge to the north. From there he could scan the country and tell if any large parties were headed their direction.

On the windswept rise, he could see the dust in the west. Obviously that was from the large main herd, and he estimated it perhaps five or so miles west of their location. That also meant that if a band was coming to intercept the herd's movement, they would come right up the Canadian bottoms. He better go back and move Durant and Sugar.

When Slocum rose to his knees, the hard south wind swept his face. Several killdeer called sharply. He worried about Durant's weakened condition. No matter. They needed to move. He stuck the scope in his saddlebags, mounted the gray, and headed back.

"What is it?" she asked when he reined the gray up.

"The main herd is west of us. We best head out of here." He glanced at Durant, who was sound asleep. "You think he can sit a horse?"

"He'll have to," she said, and began gathering their camp things.

"What's wrong?" Durant asked in a weak voice.

"Rest," Slocum said, and ran to get the mule.

"I can help. . . ."

"Lie down," she said sharply. Durant gave a shrug and obeyed her.

In fifteen minutes, the panniers were in place, horses saddled, and they shared the fresh coffee. Slocum listened to the wind whipping the willows. At least it would be at their backs, but it was strong enough that he had little doubt that it was bringing in a weather change.

They helped Durant in the saddle. He made a show of gusto, but the grayness of his face under the whisker stubble worried Slocum. Sugar rushed off to mount her horse, and brought the loaded mule back with her.

Slocum led the way with Durant between them. They soon left the bottoms and made the rise to the north. Durant managed to stay in the saddle going up the steep grade.

"See anything?" he asked, joining Slocum, who studied their back trail and anything out of the ordinary in the bottoms.

"No, but my skin was itching back there."

Durant nodded woodenly, but did not bother to look around. He grasped the saddle horn cap, acting as if all his efforts were directed to staying in the saddle. Ready to ride, Slocum shared a sharp look with Sugar. He sent the gray northward in a long trot.

Clouds began to build up in the south. High towering ones that spelled rain, forcing him to turn occasionally and check them. At midday the riders stopped, and Slocum helped Durant off his horse. Sugar rode off, and Durant used his roan for a prop while he drained his bladder.

"Sorry I'm holding you up," he said in a coarse voice.

"You ain't bothering me. So we don't run into the Indians, is all I'm concerned about."

"Yeah, but you wanted to stop that gun trade."

"That—we may be too late to do it anyway."

"Hell—" Durant fell into a fit of coughing, and barely managed to get his pants rebuttoned. Then he dropped to his knees and waved Slocum away as he choked out, "I'll make it."

He regained his feet and stood drunkenly beside the horse. Sugar rode up and gave him a wry look.

"You sure you can do this?" she asked.

"Damn right," he said, and tried to remount. His effort failed, and Slocum helped him back in the saddle.

"I smell rain," she said, and twisted around.

"It's coming back there. Better get out our slickers," Slocum said aboard his gray, observing the sheets of rain streaking the sky on their back trail. He undid Durant's slicker and helped him in it. Then he shrugged on his own. He nodded to her under the canvas poncho, then took the lead and they headed north.

The rumble of thunder rolled over the land, and the wind-driven drops pelted Slocum's rubber raincoat. Grateful the storm was to their backs, he dropped off the ridge, hoping to make less of a target for the lightning that danced over them. All they needed was a strong storm. He twisted around and checked on Durant. He was still in the saddle, but this weather would tax him even more. Slocum turned back, hoping his sense of direction was holding and he wasn't circling around in the grayness of midday.

Soon pellets of ice began to hammer on his hat and dance off his shoulders. Hail could be as large as a man's head in this country. He felt grateful that so far the hail had been small. The flashes of the grave diggers, a name that the Texas trail drovers called lightning, darted and streaked over and around them. An occasional one crashed into the earth nearby and made the very ground under his horse shake.

"Should we stop?" she asked above the downpour. Her face was flushed with rain despite the hat.

"Best keep moving. Long as he can stand it," Slocum said, loud enough for her to hear him. He ducked instinctively at the nearby clap of thunder.

She nodded, and dropped back to ride beside Durant.

Slocum turned back to the way ahead. As long as Durant made it, they'd push on, but who knows how long Durant's strength would last? Slocum closed his eyes to the misery of the downpour. A shiver ran up his spine, causing goose-flesh on the backs of his arms. Where was the gunrunner? By this time they were no doubt too late, and Black Horn had the rifles. Damn. He shut his eyelids for a moment to escape the onslaught of the storm and reality.

23

"Going to come a rain." Whitney pointed to the south at the high bank of thunderheads.

Vin nodded. He had halfway expected Raven to come back with word from Black Horn. At first he hadn't believed she'd run off with that horny kid, the way the note said. But when she didn't return, he'd grown more apprehensive that the note was telling the truth.

This Blue Song, or whatever her name was, was not like Raven under the covers. He had managed to enter her only by force. And he hadn't been able to arouse her. She had simply lain there the whole time. It had kind of killed the fun for him. That potbellied little Comanche bitch was lots more fun that this good-looking one in bed.

Maybe if he had some whiskey, that would loosen her up. He could use some himself.

"Tie down that canvas good, boys," the old man ordered. The two brothers scrambled around to fix down the wagon cover. Vin headed back for his own wagon. He glanced at the darkening sky. If he staked down the large cover over his rig, then he and Blue Song could crawl underneath it and ride out the weather. Most rain didn't last long. The notion of having her under there made him feel better. Let it storm.

Vin found his ax and began to make stakes from the supply of wood in his wagon. He occasionally looked up at the distant rumble. The squaw was seated on the ground, busy with her beadwork.

"Get off your ass and help me," he shouted to her.

She frowned, then rose and came over. On his knees he beat the first stake into the ground with the side of the ax, then indicated for her to get to the edge of the wagon tarp and tie it down. Obviously, she knew about such things, for she soon had the corner roped down. He drove in another, and the wind began to pop the tarp. He hurried to the back, and Blue Song tied down the next corner, fighting with the wind to draw it down. Soon he had the wagon covered.

With a small shovel, he began to dig a trench around the upper side. She moved their things under the wagon. If there was enough time, he could keep the water from coming under it. A fresh mist of rain struck him as he grubbed at the tough roots and cut a V ditch as quickly as he could. With new speed he sliced his way. Then a nearby bolt of thunder clapped, and he ducked his head. Enough digging. He threw down the spade and dove under the wagon's cover.

When he was underneath the wagon box at last, the storm began to drum on the canvas over him. In the gray darkness, he saw her sitting cross-legged. Good, his bedroll was under there. He knocked his hat off on the underside of the wagon floor. In disgust, he glanced at the low ceiling, then set his hat aside. With a small smile on his face, he curled his finger at her to come over to him.

She came on her hands and knees. He admired the long fringe on her blouse. The thoughts of squeezing her firm pear-shaped breasts again made his dick stiffen. This time it would be different. He went over and dug out a pint of rye from his things.

Crawling back, he looked into her brown eyes and grinned. "I got the medicine for you, sweet ass."

He removed the cork with his teeth, then shoved the bottle to her. "Drink up, darling."

She drew back and shook her head.

"I said, drink it!"

"No—"

"Don't tell me no!" He drew back his fist and hit her. The force of the blow spilled her on the ground. Like a cat he was on top of her, forcing the whiskey into her mouth, and then holding her nose between the fingers of his other hand and forcing her to swallow. She came up coughing and out of breath.

"Drink it!" he demanded, shoving the bottle at her.

She glared at him, then took the bottle. She threw her head back, took a deep swallow, and came up sputtering from the sharp whiskey.

He grinned in satisfaction over his accomplishment. "Now drink the rest. I'll show you a few things."

Thunder pealed over the wagon, and sounded so close, the very earth beneath them shook for a few seconds. He hated lightning. He knew men who had been struck dead by it. For a moment, he tried to remember how to ward it off, but the remedy escaped him. He pushed down his galluses, and then sat down on his butt to remove his pants, already contemplating sticking it to her.

Then, when the next bolt of thunder struck, she surged past him and out from under the wagon. He jumped up, too late to stop her, struck his head on the wagon box, and with his britches around his ankles found himself sprawled facedown on the grass.

"Gawdamn you!" he swore, jerking up his pants. With his galluses finally up, all he could think about was how to stop her. He rushed out into the deluge. Thick rain swept his hatless face, so he couldn't see ten feet.

"Come back here, you bitch!" he shouted, but in his storm-slashed world, he saw no sign of her.

"I'll teach you a lesson you won't ever forget!" he screamed above the wind and lashing water.

Soon the icy rain began to penetrate his shirt and shoulders. It was no use, she was gone, and he couldn't do anything but duck down from streaks of blinding light smashing the sky. How would he ever trade with Black Horn without her? Raven was gone. Now the other one. He closed his eyes and turned back to the wagon.

"Go on, you dumb bitch! You weren't worth a damn in bed anyway," Vin shouted in vain at the wind. On his hands and knees he crawled back inside the shelter, his knees wet and cold from the rain. When he found her, he would beat her butt bloody. She'd know to never run off on him again. He clenched his chattering teeth to the chill seizing him and listened to the powerful storm outside.

Slocum turned in the saddle. They were headed off a rise, and he wondered if Durant was awake enough to hang on. The hard rain, after several hours, had begun to break up. A warm breath of wind swept his face. The steady drizzle gave way, and the sky threatened to let in some light. A half-dozen killdeer ran screaming ahead of them.

"You all right?" he asked, reining his gray in beside the buckskin.

Durant nodded and grunted. Slocum looked at him hard, then exhaled.

"We can stop and rest."

Durant waved that away.

"Your ass, not mine," Slocum said, and started downhill. Ahead, something lay to the side of their path, and he narrowed his eyelids to make out the form.

"That a body?" Sugar asked, pulling her horse in close to him.

"Looks like it," he said, opening his coat to reach his gun butt and looking around to be certain it was not a trap.

"It's an Indian," she said, and dismounted. Dropping the reins, she started for the form on the ground before Slocum could warn her.

"My Gawd, it's a girl and she's freezing to death," she declared.

Still apprehensive, Slocum dismounted, catching Durant's horse to stop him, the Colt in his other hand. It would be real easy to step into a trap; he craned his head around to check.

"She's freezing, Slocum," Sug said, kneeling down beside the girl.

"Get her undressed and out of those wet clothes," he said, and holstered the .44. Still wary, he undid the bedroll from behind the saddle. "We'll get her inside this and try to warm her is all I know to do."

When he reached Sug's side, she had removed the blouse, and the shivering girl was hugging her firm brown breasts to her body. With the slick wet skirt off her, he helped Sug roll her inside the bedroll. The Indian girl's eyes looked glazed, as if she was dizzy.

"She's drunk too," Sug said to him with a concerned frown.

"Drunk?" He could hardly believe her.

"Smell her breath if you don't believe me."

"I believe you." But how in the hell did she get drunk out here by herself? At the sound of hooves, he quickly turned to see a piebald horse come over the hill and nicker at their animals. Then the horse came down the slope in a long trot to join the others.

"That might be how she got here," Sug said.

They both twisted around at Durant's groan. In a rush they hurried over to catch him as he slumped over the saddle horn. They eased him off the horse. Slocum shook his head. Now they had two sick people to manage. What next?

"We need to build a fire," Sug said, looking about.

"All the chips we could gather will be too wet to burn after all this rain," he said. "No wood closer than the Canadian that I can recall."

She agreed as she knelt beside the half-conscious Durant. "We best get him inside a bedroll too."

Slocum agreed. He jerked Durant's bedding free of the saddle strings and unfurled it. Busy spreading it out, he turned at Sug's gasp, and his hand reached for his gun butt.

"Riders coming!" she said, scrambling to her feet.

Slocum blinked. It was Don Reyas and two of his guards.

"It's okay, they're my friends," he said.

"Yes, the Comanchero. I remember him."

"Ah, Slocum, what are you doing here?" Don Reyas asked as he dismounted and shed his gloves to shake hands.

"Long story. You know Sugar. That's Sam Durant, who's under the weather, and we have one chilled squaw over here."

"You have a hospital here?" Reyas asked, and grinned. "What can I do to help you?"

"How far away is your train?"

"Not far. I will send for a wagon and we can carry them to my camp. Perhaps we can cure their ills."

"You are an angel in disguise," Slocum said.

Reyas waved that away, and sent one of his riders after a conveyance for the patients. The man rushed off on horseback, and soon disappeared over the hillside.

"How has the trading been going?" Slocum asked.

"Good, my friend. We are heading back to New Mexico. Our wagons are full of hides and we have not met any bad hostiles."

"Good. Have you seen a man calls himself Malloy?"

"Ah, yes. He is a buffalo hunter?"

"I'm not certain, but I think he has repeaters to sell to Black Horn."

"You think so?" Reyas's eyes narrowed with concern.

"Yes. He was supposed to deliver forty some Winchesters to Gilbert's store at Ft. Supply. Instead of doing that, he headed out here looking for Black Horn. He must know the Comanche has money."

"I met him two days ago with some buffalo hunters named Whitney."

"Had he sold his rifles?"

Reyas shrugged. "I don't know about that, but I doubt he would still have been out here if he had."

"That's right. Could you give me directions?"

"Better yet, me and some of my men would ride with you over there."

"Don't count me out," Durant managed in a hoarse voice. "I want that cuss's hide. He's the reason that I'm in this shape."

"We'll see," Slocum said, squatting down on his boot heels. He drew up a long stem of grass and chewed on it. Was there still time to stop the trade? He wished he knew for certain.

24

"Malloy! Malloy!" Grant shouted outside the wagon. "Them damn Injuns're coming to trade. You better get your ass out here quick-like."

With his head ducked under the wagon box ceiling, Vin pulled on his damp boots. "I'm coming. I'm coming. You sure it's them?"

When he stuck his head out, he noticed the ragged clouds tearing northward. Rain must be over, he decided, and put up his galluses. Then he saw the line of riders. He could make out about two dozen of them, coming on paints and piebalds.

"Don't get excited," he said to Grant. "That looks like Black Horn leading them."

"He speak English?" Grant asked as they hurried up to the Whitney wagon.

Vin nodded.

"Collie, you and Grant," the old man ordered, looking wild-eyed about the approaching bucks. "You two get all them rifles and ammo up here. Malloy's guns too. I don't want some buck stealing any of it." He spat aside, then turned to Vin and asked, "That the one you been waiting on?"

"That's him," Vin said, wishing he didn't feel like a man on the verge of a diarrhea attack. His guts roiled like a drowning snake.

"I don't see very many gawdamn hides," the old man complained.

"There will be. Trust me."

"I been doing that and it ain't got me diddly-shit. There better be a big pile of them at the end of this deal," Whitney warned.

"There will be." Vin set out to intercept the Comanche chief, who rode with a buffalo hide slung over his shoulder.

"Where is woman?" Black Horn asked, reining his stallion up and suspiciously looking over their camp.

"She run off yesterday. She didn't come back to you?"

Black Horn shook his head in disapproval. His long greasy hair shone in the dazzling sunshine piecing through the cloud cover.

"You come to buy rifles?" Vin asked.

"How many?"

"Two for each brave here."

Black Horn's cruel smile etched his full lips. He leaped from his horse with the Winchester, coated with brass tacks, in his hand.

"You have that many rifles?" He tried to look past Vin as the Whitneys hurried to display the rifles.

"She said you had much money and hides for them."

Black Horn nodded. Then his black eyes cut around and he glared at Vin. "How many hides?"

"Fifty." Vin knew he needed that many skins to keep the Whitneys happy. He waited for the chief's reply. His stomach curdled and the sourness rose behind his tongue. He was face-to-face with a stinking boar buck that had probably killed a hundred white men, and only Gawd knows how many white women and girls that he'd raped.

"Fifty hides?"

"Yes, fifty." He wondered if the red bastard could even count.

"You have bullets?"

"Plenty of ammo."

"Fifty hides?" Black Horn asked again as if considering the amount.

"Yeah, fifty hides and that money chest." Vin wondered if the Comanche even knew what he meant about the number.

Black Horn looked critically at the array of weapons. He put his own rifle down and checked the action on several of the Winchesters. With a large-bladed knife from his belt, he pried open the top of one of the wooden ammo boxes, removing a cartridge package. Then a smile creased his hard face as he spilled the bright brass shells into his hand. The wind snapped the canvas on Whitney's wagon. Somewhere some ravens cawed. Finally the chief nodded his head in approval.

He rose and picked up his own weapon. Then he spoke loudly in Comanche to the line of bucks on horseback. He drew their hard-faced nods of approval and a few loud hoots. He stalked to his stallion, bounded aboard, then pushed him in close to Vin.

"Be back at sundown." Black Horn's dark eyes bored a hole through Vin.

"I'll have them," Vin said.

Black Horn turned and motioned for the bucks to follow. They left yipping like a pack of coyotes. Vin felt a deep hard pressure on his bladder. He walked right by Whitney, and with a glance back to be certain the Indians weren't looking, undid his pants and pissed a fiery streak.

Finished at last, he leaned on the wagon and caught his breath. Hell, those had been the toughest moments in his entire life, facing that redskin and living to talk about it.

"I heard you say fifty hides out there to him," the old man whined. "You told us hundreds of hides."

"Them fifty's for you all."

"What's your part of the deal?"

"He's paying me."

"Paying you? How did a gawdamn Injun get any money?"

"Must have borrowed it at a bank." Vin said, and laughed. It made him feel better. But his heart still raced, and he quickly dried his clammy hands on his damp pants.

Good thing that Black Horn's dumb slut Raven had run off somewhere with that soft-pecker kid. Thinking about her brown butt made him mad. The fact that the Cheyenne woman was not there either to stick his dick into also chafed him. He'd find some sluts in Dodge when he got up there, but in six weeks he'd be back in St. Louis with tubs of money. Maybe he should go west instead of east. That freighter Arney might be wise to the fact that he'd never delivered the guns to Ft. Supply. West was where he'd head as soon as he closed the deal.

In a few hours. All he had to do was wait. And to worry about a possible double cross from those dumb Whitneys or that dangerous Comanche. It would be a long grueling time until sundown.

Slocum sat on his boot heels. His boots were still sodden. Jiminez brought him coffee. He looked up and thanked the older man.

"Who's the Cheyenne woman?" the cook asked.

"Don't know. We found her freezing to death."

"And the wounded one?"

"That's Sam Durant. He tangled with that gunrunner in Ft. Dodge. Got himself shot and took an infection."

"Pedro is a good man with wounds. He says he will recover."

"Thanks," Slocum said, grateful to have the news. No doubt Sug would be pleased for she had taken a strong concern for Durant's welfare. Slocum was left with what he could do about the arms sales. If he could do anything. *Too late* rang in his brain.

"They say your friend is talking," Reyas said, joining him.

Slocum grinned and nodded. "He could talk the leg off a big horse. How is the Indian woman we found?"

"Drinking hot coffee and she's finally stopped shaking. A very attractive one."

"Perhaps we should ask her about the gun deal?"

Reyas nodded.

"How many were there with Malloy?"

"Oh, four Whitneys and him. Five altogether."

Slocum rose to his feet, finished the coffee, and stretched his arms over his head. Damp weather made him stiff. He needed to get moving. With Reyas on his heels, they went to the tent set up for the two patients.

"Slocum, look at him," Sug announced proudly when they entered the tent.

"By damn, Durant, you may live yet."

The man blinked his eyes, sitting cross-legged on the blanket. "Hey, all because of you two. Whew, that was the damned longest ride of my life."

"You going to tell him?" she asked with an edge of impatience in her voice.

"Sure, I was getting to it," Durant said. "Sug and I are getting married."

"Wonderful."

"You'll be my best man?"

"If I can. I'd be honored to, but—"

"Yeah, we know," Sam said, and reached out to hug her.

"You can do it at my ranch," Reyas said.

"Thanks," Durant said, and shared a nod of approval with her.

"Where is the Indian?" Slocum asked.

"She must have gone outside," Sug said, looking around the sunlight-flooded tent.

Slocum nodded and went outside. He spotted the Indian woman sitting on the ground, redoing her braids at some distance from the tent and wagons.

"Speak English?" he asked.

She never looked at him, but nodded. As she was busy

doing her right braid, he noticed her shapely figure under the beaded buckskins.

"Who were you running from?"

"White men."

"Where are your people?"

"My man is dead," she said, as if that explained enough for him.

"You're mourning?"

She nodded.

"These men buffalo hunters?"

"May-loy."

"Does he still have the rifles in boxes?" His heart raced at his discovery.

"Yes." She nodded and looked at him questioningly.

"Good," he said. "I needed to know that and need to stop him." He hurried off to find Reyas. There still might be time to prevent the sale. If a few of Reyas's men would ride with him, possibly they could take the weapons back before they fell into Comanche hands. He didn't have much time.

25

Vin sat on the ground. The low light from the chip fire illuminated the wagon side. It was long past sundown and no sign of the damn Comanche. Had Black Horn made another deal with some other trader? Like those lying Mexicans who'd gone through—he'd bet they sold those red bastards guns. No telling about the belligerent devil. No way anyone else had this many new rifles, unless they'd robbed a store or shipment as he had. Lucky thing for him that Arney bunch wanted to get back to St. Louis so bad, they'd hired him to deliver the rifles.

"Where's that red-ass bastard?" the old man asked.

"Injuns don't have clocks in their heads," Vin said sharply.

"I want to get the hell out of here. Figure every day we stay here is one more big chance we're taking on having our scalps lifted."

"He'll be coming. Them fifty robes I'm asking for ain't that easy to get at once."

"Why, he should have hundreds of them."

"Maybe, maybe not."

"Well, shit, if he's got to go get them—I mean, kill them—it could be another week."

"Whitney, you're getting your skins, stop bitching at me."

"I just get—"

"So do we all. If your dumb son hadn't run off with that little whore, we'd have her to answer our questions."

"Well, I damn sure never told him to do that stupid trick. Fact was, he was the smartest one of the three. Good with numbers, my, my." The old man shook his head ruefully. "That boy could sure count."

Vin was too busy thinking in his own mind how he would handle the money. Put it in panniers and strap them on his mule with a packsaddle. He would want to move faster than the wagon would go when he finally got it from the Comanche. He'd head south, then swing west. He could almost feel those coins in his fingers.

It sure would be great to be rich.

"I'm turning in. Them injuns ain't coming tonight," the old man said, and his two sons agreed.

"I'll wait up awhile," Vin said with his back to the wagon wheel.

His eyes half open, Vin lurched to his feet. They were coming in the golden light of dawn. He could see the horses pulling travois being led by women. The travois were piled high with robes. He must have fallen asleep during the night with his back to the wagon wheel. His fortune was coming.

He started to get the rifles displayed, then stopped in his tracks. "Get your asses up. He's coming with the robes!" Then, not waiting for the grumbling replies from about the camp where the Whitneys lay in their bedrolls, he began lining the rifles up.

Black Horn rode up on his foot-stamping stallion. The big stud ran his spotted dick out several times, hunched his powerful butt, and finally ejaculated. The big tool quickly dissolved, but a foot and half of it hung limp under his belly.

The stern-faced chief nodded in approval at the weapons. He dismounted, and a squaw rushed up and took the reins. She used two hands to hold the prancing stud, who bobbed his head and curled back his lips, testing the air.

Black Horn picked up the first new rifle and worked the action. Then he nodded without a word, and started back toward the line of travois. Women began piling the woolly robes in stacks of ten. Soon they had them unloaded in five stacks. Then two of them strained to bring over the familiar-looking strongbox.

Vin's heart ran away. He caught his short breath. When Black Horn used the new rifle muzzle to flip back the lid, the sun shone on the mountain of silver and gold coins. A damn fortune was in there. A million things ran through Vin's mind. He would never skin another stinking buffalo ever again. He'd hire someone to do it, maybe, but he wouldn't have to.

"Where is woman?" Black Horn demanded.

Vin shook his head, coming back from his daydreams. "Gone. She ran away." He threw his arms up in surrender.

Black Horn nodded. He motioned for the women to begin loading the rifles and the ammunition on the travois. Vin quickly nodded, and shut the lid on the strongbox.

"What we going to do with all that money?" the old man whispered excitedly from behind him.

"Hold on to your guns," Vin said under his breath. Though he doubted Black Horn would do anything with the women there, the deal wouldn't be over until the Indians rode out.

Black Horn swung aboard his stallion. He came back to Whitney's wagon.

"Need more guns," he said.

"You got more money and robes?" Vin asked. His heart was racing so fast he feared his knees would buckle.

"Get more. When you bring more guns and bullets?" The chief's coal-colored eyes glared at him like drills.

"This fall," Vin lied. If the sumbitch thought he could

get more guns and ammunition then, he wouldn't stop or harm them now. It was Vin's ticket to safe passage. "When the geese fly," he promised.

"Geese fly, meet you on the Canadian," Black Horn said.

"Yes, yes," Vin said, overcome with the idea that he could stop worrying about the Comanches killing him.

The rasp of the loaded travois sticks on the ground sounded like music. Vin watched them ride away. The blanket-wearing fish-eyed bucks and the dirty raggedly dressed squaws were leading the horses away. He drew a deep breath, and his shoulders sagged in relief.

"How much money we got there, *partner?*" the old man asked from behind him.

Slocum saddled his gray on the picket line. He looked up and saw the Cheyenne woman coming toward him. The breeze was swinging the long fringe of her skirt and sleeves. Her firm breasts rocked under the fancy beadwork of her long-sleeved blouse. A real tribal princess, he decided, and reached under the horse to pull up the girth. Some buck must have given a horse herd to her father for her hand in marriage. The one that she said was dead.

"Are you leaving?" she asked.

"Yes."

"Where will you go?"

"I'm going to check on this Malloy. I want to stop the sale of his guns to the Comanches."

"I will go with you."

"It could be dangerous. Why do you wish to go?"

"I want to see him die."

"He hurt you?" Slocum waited for her answer before he finished threading the leather down.

She nodded.

"I may not kill him," Slocum said, turning to the task. Finished, he shook the saddle by the horn to be certain it was on good.

"Then *I* will," she said.

He agreed with a sharp nod. Whatever Malloy had done to her, he'd probably live to regret it. The main thing was to stop the gun trade—if Slocum wasn't too late.

"What do your people call you?" he asked.

"Blue Song."

"Slocum," he said, and she acknowledged his name. In a bound, he was on the gray. He looked down at her. "You may come along. I can't promise you anything."

She nodded, and ran off for her piebald horse.

Reyas and five of his toughest men joined him. They were all well armed as they started for the gunrunner's last camp. The Cheyenne woman trailed them. Slocum saw that that was where she wanted to be, and set the rested gray into a long lope.

A red-tailed hawk screamed at their intrusion. He dipped low over them, his white underbelly fluffed by the wind. Then he swung away and soared on the updraft. His shrill voice carried across the rolling prairie in angry challenge.

At midday they spotted camp smoke. Slocum used his telescope to scan the village from afar.

"Comanche, Kiowa, or Cheyenne?" Reyas asked, bellied down beside him.

"Comanche, it looks like from here." Slocum saw no artwork on the gray skin walls. The women about camp appeared dressed in dirt-colored clothing.

"Can you tell anything else?"

"No." He rolled over and waved the Cheyenne woman forward. She came on the run and dropped down beside him. He handed her the scope.

"Here, take a look. Do you recognize the camp?"

She peered through the scope. Then nodded. "Black Horn's."

"He there?" Reyas asked.

She took the eyepiece away and shook her head. "Warriors gone."

"Means we may be too late," Reyas said with a grim set to his thin mouth.

Slocum agreed. Too late . . . he had halfway expected that ever since he had heard about the rifle sales. Black Horn could be out already making a serious raid with the new arms.

"Guess it's time we reconsider our plans," Slocum said. "He may have those arms."

Reyas agreed solemnly. "But this greedy man who sells them will cause much grief for innocent people. He should be punished."

"Fine. We'll capture him and give him to the authorities in Ft. Supply."

"Will they listen to us?" Reyas asked.

"We aren't judge and jury."

Reyas gave a shrug. "Sometimes the gringo law is not so good."

"I agree, but it is the right way. Much as I hate him for what he did, it isn't my way to summarily execute him."

"What if he won't surrender?"

"Then he chooses to die."

"Good. We will ride with you and find this man."

Slocum rose, took the telescope, and pulled the Cheyenne woman to her feet. The three ran for their horses. It wasn't over yet.

Vin spent the afternoon stewing over what he must do. He was taking that money when he left. Those Whitneys could die in hell before he gave them a share. The greedy bastards had five hundred dollars or more in the hides. But they wanted the money too.

He could tell from where he sat on the ground, pinching out small bunches of grass between his thumb and forefinger and throwing them to the wind, that the Whitneys were armed and ready. Those two boys were sporting sidearms in their waistbands. Some old cap-and-ball pistols. It would be lucky if they'd even fire. It was the old man Vin figured would be the toughest to gun down.

He rose to his feet, dried his sweaty palms on his

britches, and crossed the distance to their campfire. Smoke swirled around on the wind and smarted his eyes when he squatted down to get himself some coffee.

"How we splitting the money?" the old man asked, busy whittling on a cedar branch.

"We got to take out my expenses first," Vin said, setting the pot back down and putting the kerchief he'd used for a pot holder in his back pocket.

"How much is that? You stole them Winchesters."

"It costed me plenty. Besides, they ain't looking for you boys."

The old man grinned. "Right, it's your ass they want for doing that."

Vin agreed. He rose and considered their positions. The old man sat on the tongue shaving off red curls with his Barlow. Grant was resting with his back to the front wheel. Collie was busy fixing some harness so they could pull out for civilization come first light.

Vin finished the cup of coffee, satisfied he had the edge he needed. He dropped the cup and drew the new Colt he'd taken off the sodbuster. He aimed at the shocked old man and fired. Hit hard, Whitney pitched off the wagon tongue to the ground. Then Vin deliberately swung the barrel toward Grant and took him in the face at point-blank range. Collie had scrambled for a rifle. Without hesitation, Vin shot the boy twice, once in the middle of his back, then in the back of the head. The boy went limp facedown.

Short of breath, Vin felt his eyes smart from the gun smoke. With quaking hands, he punched out the empties and reloaded. Both boys were still as he stepped over Collie's body and went to see about the old man.

Sprawled on his back, Whitney showed his gritted yellow teeth when Vin came around the wagon to find him. "Damn you double-crossing liar!" the old man managed.

Vin shot him twice more. "Your trouble, Whitney, is you was too damn greedy!"

Quickly he reloaded. Butterflies danced in his stomach.

He searched the sea of grass and saw nothing. Then a sharp cramp in his gut told him he needed to drop his pants and quick. Another endless hot flush of diarrhea left him weak-kneed. He fought back the nausea of vomiting and went for his animals. He'd need to pack the money on the mule. A wagon would be far too slow. Maybe one of their mules would beat his own to use as a pack animal. He went, caught a large black one from their team, and led him back.

The skin on the back of his neck crawled. Any minute he expected someone to ride up. The shrill cry of a plover caused him to drop the packsaddle and whirl around. He couldn't stay there. Besides, he hated dead bodies. Finally, he had the animal saddled, and led him to the strongbox. It was too heavy to put on one side.

He rushed off to look for panniers. He would need to divide it. His heart was pounding, and a deep headache was drumming in his temples. Midway to his own wagon, his guts began to knot, and he was forced to drop his pants or risk an accident. This time it felt like he passed a flush of hot water. Wearily, he finally rose and pulled up his galluses. Damn, there was something wrong with him.

With the panniers on the mule at last, he began, a double handful at time, to move the double eagles and silver cartwheels from the box to the pack. It was hard work and his hands shook, which made him spill some on the ground. No time to waste. At last he had half the coins in one side, and dragged the box around to the other side of the mule to fill that side.

He spoke sharply to the animal when it stomped hard at a heel fly. No time. No time for foolishness from that mule, that was for certain. He finished and mopped his feverish face on his sleeve, resting for a moment against the mule. The shits had sure made him weak.

He tied the mule to the back wagon wheel and hurried to find Clunny. Filled with dread over the lack of his own strength, he dragged the sorrel back to his wagon. It required super strength for him to saddle Clunny. His arms pained him as he tossed the rig on the horse's back. He went to his knees, reaching under for the girth, and staggered up.

Then the world tilted. He fought for his bearings, then staggering every step, led the horse to the mule. Again the lightning pains of distress forced him to undo his pants. He used a hand on the wagon wheel to keep himself from falling over as the fiery ravages of his loose bowels threatened to set his butt on fire. The pain made his jaw muscles draw tight and cramp.

At last he mounted, jerked the mule's lead rope, pulled his head up from grazing, and headed south. He needed to make lots of tracks. Bleary-eyed, he forced Clunny and the mule to trot. But he soon ran out of strength and had to let them walk, until he could draw up enough energy to make them do it.

By late afternoon, he could see the cottonwoods that marked the Canadian. Maybe he'd rest awhile there. Dizzy-headed, he sent Clunny off the escarpment, and headed for the silver stream glistening in the late afternoon sun.

He looked forward to a cool drink too. His guts were still at war and his mouth tasted like a barefoot tribe had marched through it. The fever made him light-headed, and he started to lose his bearings. Bad time for him to feel this bad.

He dropped from the saddle heavily under the fluttering cottonwoods. Their leaves were rattling overhead in the afternoon wind. Some ravens protested his invasion. He hobbled the mule which was loaded with his precious cargo, satisfied that Clunny wouldn't stray.

He recalled stumbling to the water's edge and dropping down. On his hands and knees he splashed some water in his face. Then he bellied down on the ground to get himself a drink. He awoke spitting water. He must have passed out and fallen face-first into it. Too weak to rise, he crawfished backward on the sand. Then he fainted again.

"How did you get that mule?" Vin woke up and all he could see was the muzzle of his own .45 stuck in his eye. Someone had him hauled up by the shirtfront and was demanding answers.

"Tell me, Malloy!"

Vin could see it was the youngest Whitney. He had no way to fight him. His arms and legs felt powerless. Why didn't Malcolm go away?

"Injuns attacked us," he finally managed.

"When?"

"This morning—noontime. It was hell, we fought hard. Only thing left was Clunny and that mule."

"You mean my brothers and Paw are dead?"

"Yeah, couldn't do nothing for them." Vin waited, hoping the boy bought his lies. It was his only chance. He fought the gagging under his tongue. It threatened to choke him, and he pushed the kid's hands away to vomit.

Malcolm stepped back to get out of the way, still holding the gun on him. Vin's eyes ran from the burning stench and he heaved again. Some flew out his nose and seared his nostrils. He gulped for air.

"Injuns . . . must have been Cheyennes." He gasped for his breath.

"You bury them?" Malcolm sounded taken aback by the news.

Good, the boy was buying his story. Now he had to catch him off guard. The terrible sour taste in Vin's mouth forced him to gag again.

"Did the best I could." Vin huffed for more air. His thoughts filled with the dread that there might be more inside his guts that needed out.

"So where were you going?" Malcolm demanded.

Vin sat back on his butt. He tried to focus on the boy's face. He wondered where the slut Raven was.

Then he saw her bringing a handful of his coins to show Malcolm.

"Black Horn's money," she said, and gave Vin a look of disdain.

"It is," Vin said, and dropped his head. If he could only sleep a few hours. "We were going to head back to Ft. Supply tomorrow . . . when they attacked us."

Malcolm nodded, then frowned and motioned at Vin's stomach. "What's wrong with you?"

"Got the bellyache like I been poisoned. Had it for a while."

"Where are you headed?"

"Anywhere away from them renegades."

"How did you escape and they didn't?"

"How should I know? We fought them a few hours. Almost ran out of ammo. Your paw was first one shot. He took a Sharps bullet a-sitting on the wagon tongue, whittling. Me, Collie, and Grant dove under the wagon. We held them off for a while. Then a stray arrow got Grant in the throat. It was bad. Nothing we could do. Him gurgling and blood running all over the place. Me and Collie, we cut down some of them bucks in the next charge.

"A bullet right between the eyes took him out. He never suffered. Them Cheyenne rode off. Must have been five of them red bastards down out there. The rest pulled out for no reason I could figure, so I real quick-like saddled up and rode like hell to get here."

Malcolm uncocked the Colt and put it in his waistband. "I ain't sure I believe ya, but you're sick sure enough. How much money you got on that mule?"

"Never counted it."

"I will," he said, and went to the mule. The girl helped him unload it. Helpless, Vin lay with his head on the grass, his stomach kicking him like a jackass. He was forced to watch the boy with his treasure and unable to do a thing about it.

"Whew, there must be a fortune in here," Malcolm said, sounding impressed.

He and Raven ignored Vin. Malcolm busied himself

counting and stacking coins. Vin passed in and out of consciousness. Once he awoke and spat some dry grass from his mouth. The money counting continued. He needed some Black Draught remedy. It would cure this belly sickness, but he was miles from a store that sold it. Boiled blackberry root tea worked on things like this. There were none of those bushes in this bottom. Besides, he was too weak to hold his head up, let alone dig roots.

"There's way over two thousand dollars here," Malcolm gushed.

The lights went out again for Vin. He pitched off into the darkness.

26

"You reckon we could ride down there and take those children back?" Slocum asked, considering the Comanche village.

"They might kill them if they even thought we would," Reyas warned.

"You're probably right."

They mounted up and skirted the camp. Reyas felt certain they would reach Malloy's camp by sundown. He led them northeast.

The sun was low in the west when they caught sight of the two wagons. Slocum rose in the stirrups to view it. No smoke, no activity—his hand rested on his gun butt.

"Something ain't right," Slocum said. "It might be an Indian trap."

Reyas stood up in his stirrups and agreed. His man Juarez pushed his horse in close to them.

"There isn't anything stirring down there," Reyas said to his man.

Juarez nodded with a grim look toward the two wagons. "Some of the animals are missing."

"That buzzard sees something," Slocum said, pointing to a gliding black bird of carrion. "He's going in after it too."

"Let's ride," Reyas said.

Obviously there were no Indians in hiding, or else the vultures would never have landed down there. Slocum could see there were more of them on the ground. They flapped their wings and began to rise at the men's approach.

He spotted the prone body of the old man first. He reined up the gray and dismounted. Three corpses lay strewn about.

"He is not here," Blue Song said, rushing about searching the wagons.

Slocum nodded, and then he squatted down to examine something that caught his eye. He picked up a gold twenty-dollar piece and held it up. "We're too late."

"Here." Juarez came, carrying the empty strongbox.

"That is it," Reyas said, grim-faced.

"Damn, they must of had an argument over the money," said Slocum.

"There are many fine robes here," one of the Reyas men reported. "Why did he not take them?"

"Must have gotten them out of the Comanches," Juarez said.

"I think he took the money and ran," Reyas said.

Slocum circled the camp in search of tracks. Blue Song waved him over and showed him where Malloy had loaded the money.

"He spilled more money here," she said, showing him several coins in her hand. "One of their mules is gone too. And his horse."

"Which way did he go?" Slocum asked, joining her.

She pointed south, walking in that direction and reading the sign in the grass.

"Back toward the Canadian?" he asked.

"Yes, one horse and one mule."

"I'll go back and tell Don Reyas that we're taking his trail and get our horses," Slocum said.

She looked at him hard as if she wanted to ask something, but didn't, and nodded to his words.

"Blue Song," he said. "We'll track him down."

"Good," she said, and turned back to look to the south with her hand shielding her face. The wind swept the long fringe on her skirt around her.

"So, we bury these men, load up the robes, and take them in their wagon back to the train. Perhaps they had family?" Reyas said.

"Who knows? Greed is a powerful thing," Slocum said as Reyas's men wrapped the last corpse in a piece of wagon sheet marked Arney Frieght.

"I will hold the proceeds for any claims." Reyas motioned Slocum aside. "That youngest Whitney boy is missing."

"Let's ask Blue Song," Slocum said, seeing her gathering their horses.

"The young boy?" Slocum asked her. "He is not here?"

"He went away with Raven."

Slocum turned and nodded at Reyas. "Hear her?"

"They must have left before the shooting," Reyas said, as if in deep thought.

Blue Song nodded. "They rode away before the rain."

"Saved their skins," Slocum said, and swung up in the saddle. "Amigo, she and I are taking Malloy's trail," he told Reyas. "I will see you someday in New Mexico, if not sooner."

"Be careful. Black Horn must be armed to the teeth." Reyas shook his head ruefully. "I wish I could spare some men for you."

"We'll try to dodge him and find this Malloy," Slocum said, noting Blue Song was in the saddle.

"Take some supplies," Reyas shouted after them.

Slocum waved aside his concern. He wanted to be on the killer's trail before the tracks grew any dimmer. The two of them sped across the prairie, riding into the fresh wind that swept their faces. How far away was Malloy? Slocum glanced back. He would have to avoid the Comanches too. Oh, well. He smiled at Blue Song aboard the stout

Morgan. She nodded in return, her fur-wrapped braids tossing on her shoulders as they loped southward. *Malloy, you better dig a hole and hide.*

Vin could see the stacks of money Malcolm made through his swarming vision. He needed a pistol, anything. Those two . . . that dirty-assed squaw and boy weren't taking his money! The earthquake in his burning stomach rumbled and roared. He fought back the sour bitterness from behind his tongue. If he only felt better so he could do something. He fainted away, mumbling to himself.

"How did you kill them!" Malcolm had him pulled up by the shirtfront.

"Killed who?" Vin managed, fear gripping his guts. How did that boy know he'd killed them.

"I heard you talking when you were delirious that you killed them damn Whitneys and shot them dead."

"Huh?" Vin shook his head. "Naw, I must have been out of my head. They went to Ft. Supply with over a hundred buffalo hides."

"How? You got one of their mules. Old Bob. My paw would never part with him. How could he haul them hides you been talking about without his best mule?"

Vin tried to clear his mind. The stinking smell of spent gunpowder from the barrel of the Colt held in his face didn't help none. He had to make sense.

"He took *my* mule. Lord, son, I gave him a hundred hides for their part. I traded him out of that one. Give him my mule and some money. Lord, boy, your kinfolks are rich and throwing a party at Ft. Supply."

"You're lying!"

"Nooo! I swear to Gawd, I ain't."

"You killed them!" Tears began to run down the boy's face. He let go of Vin's shirt, and Vin fell back on the ground. Then Malcolm pointed the pistol directly at Vin.

"Boy! You're wrong, they're fine," Vin said, desperate for a way to stop him from pulling the trigger. "Your folks are fine. They're—I swear to Gawd that they're in Ft.—"

The gun roared and bucked in the kid's hands. The impact of the bullet struck Vin in the chest like a sledgehammer. He tried to reach for the gun, the kid, anything. . . .

At the shot, Malcolm ran off, and began picking up handfuls of coins. Vin could see them as he strained to breathe. The damn squaw was helping him, every once in a while glancing fearfully over to see if Vin was getting up.

He had taught her lessons—big ones. If he could, he'd beat her again, twice as hard for leaving him. Through shaded vision he could see them leading the mule away. He wanted to shout at them. Stop them from taking his money. But he knew his time was running out. He could feel the blood coming out of the wound in his chest. Harder and harder to breathe. Vin turned his head sideways, and saw the two of them on horseback leading the mule and splashing across the Canadian.

"That's my money. . . ." And Vin's world went black.

Slocum and Blue Song reached the Canadian bottoms at sundown. His hand rested on his gun butt. She craned her head around, checking for signs.

They rode into a clearing, and the red rays of sunset shone on a prone body. She looked at him, and he nodded for her to go check. He took her reins, still feeling uneasy about being there. His gun hand was still ready.

"It is him," she said, kneeling beside the body. Then she rose. "He's dead. Shot. I think Raven and the boy did it. Their prints are here. They rode away." She pointed south.

He booted the gray up and looked down at the ashen face of Malloy.

"Come, we can't do anything here."

She agreed.

"Wait" someone called in a desperate hoarse voice.

Slocum whirled the gray around with the Colt in his fist. Two Indian children emerged from the willows. A boy and a girl dressed in filthy leather shirts. They looked famished.

"It's me," the boy said, his voice gravelly. "Peter Brownhouse. You know us from Black Horn's camp. We have no weapons."

Slocum holstered his gun and swung down. His breath caught in his throat. Two of those children were still alive. A miracle. He rushed over and hugged them in his arms.

"I'm Mary Martin," the girl said with a smile of relief on her dirt-streaked face.

"The others?" he asked.

He saw the looks on their faces, and knew the answer.

"How did you get away?"

"They were busy having a war dance and eating buffalo," Peter said. "We ran off."

"Good. This is Blue Song."

The two children nodded politely to her, but he read their distrust.

"No. She is my friend."

"You don't have any food, do you?" Peter asked.

"Yes, we have some jerky and I've got some hard candy. What first?" he asked, standing up.

"I'd sure like the candy," Mary said. Peter agreed.

"Good, here's some. Now, Peter, you ride behind Blue Song and hang on. Mary can ride behind me."

"Mister?" Mary asked, licking her lips before she ate the first piece. "Will you find me a dress before we find people? I mean, white people?"

"We'll sure find you a dress before then," he promised, looking around, still edgy about the willow-choked bottoms and what they might conceal. "Let's get out of here before the Comanches come looking for you."

He hoisted the boy up behind Blue Song, satisfied Peter could ride well enough to hang on to her. On the gray, he reached down, caught Mary's arm, and propelled her up behind him on the saddle.

"Hold tight," he said, and they headed out of the willow-choked bottom.

There was nothing he could do about Black Horn and the rifles, no matter how bad he felt that the Comanche had them. Let the military worry about that. Two of the four captives were freed, and sometime before the quarter moon rose high in the sky, they should find the Comancheros' camp and safety.

They paused to walk their sweating horses under the starlight.

"Where will you go next?" Blue Song asked.

"Perhaps go up in the San Juans and hunt some elk," he said as they led their animals.

"I can cook and sew," she said.

"That may be handy," he told her.

The quarter moon reached its zenith overhead as Slocum saw the Comancheros' camp. He started down the long slope, and saw someone riding out. He reined up the gray.

Why was a rider coming out? The man led something. Slocum couldn't make it out, but he made a sign for Blue Song to hold up.

"Is that the man's camp?" Peter asked in a whisper.

"Yes, it's Don Reyas's camp. He will take you to his ranch," Slocum said, still bothered. Then he recognized Juarez was leading a pack animal.

"We have watched for you," Juarez said. "Two men calling themselves sheriffs were here tonight. They asked about you."

"Did one ride an Appaloosa horse with spots on his butt?"

"*Sí.*"

"Where did they go?" Slocum asked.

"We sent them away, but Don Reyas is afraid they will watch the train for your return. He said for you to take this mule and supplies."

"I am grateful. Tell him I will repay him. These two

white children from Black Horn's camp need to go with
you."

"Oh, yes, he will be pleased," Juarez said with a smile
in the starlight. "How did you get them?"

"They ran away and we found them. Tell him Malloy is
dead. We think the Whitney boy shot him and took all the
money." Slocum hugged both of the children. "Don Reyas
will help and care for you."

"Thanks," both of them said.

Slocum felt a lump in his throat at parting with the gal-
lant pair of youngsters. Blue Song was already mounted
and had the pack mule's lead.

"Gracias, amigo," he said to Juarez, and shook the
man's hand. "Tell Don Reyas someday I will ride by and
see him." Then he turned to Blue Song. "Well, cook and
seamstress, let's go see about them elk in the high country."

She nodded, pleased, took the mule's lead, and they rode
westward.

Epilogue

Black Horn never used the repeaters in battles or raids. His entire band was wiped out four weeks later that summer by a smallpox epidemic. Malcolm Whitney and his Indian wife Raven settled in Montana. His ranching and banking interests flourished until the bitter year of '84. After the disastrous winter killed off cattle, and the nation's economy turned down later that year, Whitney fled to Canada to avoid prosecution for violations of the territorial banking laws.

JAKE LOGAN
TODAY'S HOTTEST ACTION WESTERN!

☐ SLOCUM AND THE WOLF HUNT #237	0-515-12413-3/$4.99
☐ SLOCUM AND THE BARONESS #238	0-515-12436-2/$4.99
☐ SLOCUM AND THE COMANCHE PRINCESS #239	0-515-12449-4/$4.99
☐ SLOCUM AND THE LIVE OAK BOYS #240	0-515-12467-2/$4.99
☐ SLOCUM AND THE BIG THREE #241	0-515-12484-2/$4.99
☐ SLOCUM AT SCORPION BEND #242	0-515-12510-5/$4.99
☐ SLOCUM AND THE BUFFALO HUNTER #243	0-515-12518-0/$4.99
☐ SLOCUM AND THE YELLOW ROSE OF TEXAS #244	0-515-12532-6/$4.99
☐ SLOCUM AND THE LADY FROM ABILENE #245	0-515-12555-5/$4.99
☐ SLOCUM GIANT: SLOCUM AND THE THREE WIVES	0-515-12569-5/$5.99
☐ SLOCUM AND THE CATTLE KING #246	0-515-12571-7/$4.99
☐ SLOCUM #247: DEAD MAN'S SPURS	0-515-12613-6/$4.99
☐ SLOCUM #248: SHOWDOWN AT SHILOH	0-515-12659-4/$4.99
☐ SLOCUM AND THE KETCHEM GANG #249	0-515-12686-1/$4.99
☐ SLOCUM AND THE JERSEY LILY #250	0-515-12706-X/$4.99
☐ SLOCUM AND THE GAMBLER'S WOMAN #251	0-515-12733-7/$4.99
☐ SLOCUM AND THE GUNRUNNERS #252	0-515-12754-X/$4.99
☐ SLOCUM AND THE NEBRASKA STORM #253	0-515-12769-8/$4.99
☐ SLOCUM #254: SLOCUM'S CLOSE CALL	0-515-12789-2/$4.99
☐ SLOCUM AND THE UNDERTAKER #255	0-515-12807-4/$4.99
☐ SLOCUM AND THE POMO CHIEF #256	0-515-12838-4/$4.99